Inter

FROM THE
NANCY DREW FILES

THE CASE: To find out who's behind a series of nasty accidents, Nancy must dig up a handsome ladykiller's past.

CONTACT: Nancy's friend Laurie Weaver has a big crush on a sexy dance-club deejay, which could trigger a backlash.

SUSPECTS: Jon Villiers—What does the hot new deejay have to hide?

Adam Boyd—Laurie's old boyfriend doesn't approve of her new dance partner.

Sheila Day—Jon's mysterious ex is carrying a torch that could burn both of them.

COMPLICATIONS: The teen sleuth is stepping on some toes to trip up an arsonist.

Books in The Nancy Drew Files® Series

Available from ARCHWAY Paperbacks

THE NANCY DREW FILES™ CASE · 37

LAST DANCE

Carolyn Keene

AN ARCHWAY PAPERBACK
Published by POCKET BOOKS

New York   London   Toronto   Sydney   Tokyo   Singapore

AN ARCHWAY PAPERBACK *Original*

 An Archway Paperback published by
POCKET BOOKS, a division of Simon & Schuster Inc.
1230 Avenue of the Americas, New York, NY 10020

ISBN: 0-671-74657-X

First Archway Paperback printing July 1989

10 9 8 7 6 5 4

LAST DANCE

Chapter

One

"WELL, NANCY?" Bess Marvin demanded of her friend, "is Moves the hottest dance club within a hundred miles of River Heights, or what?"

"It's great!" Nancy Drew answered, raising her voice to be heard over the music. Nancy's shoulder-length reddish blond hair took on a metallic glow as she stepped into a pool of black light. She grinned. "This is wild!"

"There's a table," George Fayne shouted, pointing to the opposite side of the club. She ran a hand through her short dark hair to fluff it and

1

strode confidently through the crowd to the table. Nancy and Bess followed.

Bess flashed a hundred-watt smile at the handsome young deejay inside the sound booth, but he didn't seem to notice her. She gave a long sigh, which made both Nancy and George grin.

"He's so gorgeous!" Bess moaned.

Nancy looked around at the club, with its black-and-white checkerboard dance floor and zebra-striped walls. Television screens hanging from the high, vaulted ceiling showed shots of the dancers, mixed with clips from music videos.

"Look, there's Julie Carlton," Bess said. "Hey, Julie!" She waved at a pretty, petite blond girl who was dancing with an enormous footballplayer type.

"Julie Carlton? Any relation to Brenda Carlton?" George asked, making a face.

"Fortunately for Julie, no." Bess laughed. "They have the same last name, but the similarity ends there. Julie's really great. How do you like this place?" she asked Julie as the girl walked up to their table.

"It's incredible," Julie answered breathlessly. "It reminds me of this club I went to in New York when I was visiting my older sister. I love all the black and white!" She grinned. "I just wish I was tall enough to see all the faces of the gorgeous guys."

Nancy laughed. "Bess knows what you're talking about," she told Julie.

Bess nodded emphatically. "It's fun to be dainty—but I know I'm going to have a stiff neck by the end of the evening," she complained.

"Julie, you deserted me." Julie's huge dancing partner strolled over just then, looking mournful. "I thought you said you'd be right back."

"Sorry, Walt," Julie said apologetically. "See you all later." She tossed the girls a wave and boogied away with Walt.

Just then a slender, pretty girl appeared at the table. She had long, glossy brown curls and a heart-shaped face. Her green eyes sparkled as she slid into the seat next to Nancy.

"Hi, everybody," she said.

"Laurie Weaver!" Nancy cried. "I haven't seen you in ages. How are you?"

Laurie had graduated the same year as Nancy and her friends at River Heights High. Although they'd never been especially close, Nancy had always liked Laurie, with her ready smile and easy sense of humor.

"I'm just fine," Laurie said. "Great, in fact. I love the summer. Listen, I'm having an outdoor party tomorrow, at five. Will you all come?"

As Nancy, George, and Bess accepted, the deejay spoke up. "This next song is for Laurie," he said. "With all my love."

Even in the dim light of the club, Nancy could see Laurie blush.

Bess's eyes widened, and she leaned forward in her chair. After casting a look at the deejay, who was gazing in their direction, she asked, "Are you the Laurie he's talking about?"

Laurie nodded. "I guess I am," she admitted with a smile.

Nancy knew that Laurie had broken up with her boyfriend, Adam Boyd, and started going with someone else a couple of weeks earlier. But it was a surprise to find out that Laurie's new guy was the deejay at Moves.

"Wow," Bess gasped. "So tell us all about him."

"His name is Jon Villiers," Laurie said. "He moved to River Heights a few months ago from Chicago to open Moves."

"Hey, Bess, come and dance with me!" A good-looking, dark-haired guy emerged from the crowd and grabbed Bess's hand. She stood up. "Don't leave—I want to hear all the details!" she yelled to Laurie as she was being towed away.

Nancy glanced at the booth and saw that someone had replaced Jon, who was moving through the crowd toward Laurie.

He seemed to be unaware of all the girls watching him and saw only Laurie. He held out his hand, and after a moment's hesitation, Laurie took it and followed him onto the dance floor.

Seconds later an angry-looking Adam Boyd charged up to Nancy's table.

"Want to dance?" he asked Nancy.

Nancy felt sorry for Adam. She knew he'd cared a lot about Laurie. The break-up had probably been hard on him. "Sure," she answered, and they moved onto the dance floor.

Adam wasn't a very attentive partner. He kept craning his neck, trying to find Laurie and Jon in the crowd. "What a couple—both losers," he said with a sneer. "You know, I lost all respect for Laurie when she fell for that Villiers creep."

Nancy sighed. "Adam—"

"He's been chasing her for weeks," Adam interrupted. "He sends her flowers, takes her to fancy restaurants for dinner, buys her expensive presents. But he's not fooling me. He's a lowlife. One of these days Laurie's going to find it out—the hard way."

Nancy was beginning to wish she hadn't accepted Adam's invitation to dance. She glanced around at Jon Villiers. He was older than she had thought at first—probably about twenty-four, and great looking, with a lean, muscular build and short, sun-bleached blond hair. His high cheekbones and perfect nose made him look like a star. Clearly, Adam was incredibly jealous of Laurie's new boyfriend, and Nancy tried to change the subject.

"Are you working in your dad's hardware store again this summer?" she asked.

Adam scowled at her and nodded. "I guess that makes me pretty dull, compared to Mr. Music there," he said, indicating Jon with his eyes. "I could tell Laurie a thing or two about him, but she won't listen. He's just after her family's money—"

Nancy looked at Adam curiously. "That's a pretty strong accusation, don't you think?" she asked.

Adam avoided Nancy's eyes for a moment. She could feel his pain and anger. "I've got to make her understand," he said in a voice so low that Nancy could barely hear him. "I've got to make Laurie see what a mistake this is."

Nancy was relieved when the dance ended and she could go back to her table. George and Bess were dancing with two of their old classmates.

Adam lingered for a moment. Nancy assumed he was waiting for Laurie to come back, but when she did start toward the table, he disappeared into the crowd.

"I saw you dancing with Adam," Laurie said to Nancy. "He's still angry with me, isn't he?"

"He'll get over it," Nancy answered, feeling a little awkward. "He needs some time, that's all."

Laurie nodded, but she didn't look convinced.

A waitress appeared. She was small, with red hair and flashing green eyes. The tag on her uniform said Pam. "Mr. Villiers said to give you this," she told Laurie in a sulky voice, handing her a note. Before Laurie could thank her, the girl was gone.

Laurie read the note, then carefully folded it and tucked it into the pocket of her jean jacket. Her smile seemed a little forced when she met Nancy's eyes. "He says there'll never be another girl for him," she said.

Something in Laurie's manner filled Nancy with concern. She leaned forward in her chair. "Laurie, what's wrong?"

Laurie swallowed. "This is all happening too fast, that's all," she confided.

Nancy waited for Laurie to go on. Instead, she changed the subject.

"Remember when we bought the same dress for that dance?" she asked.

Nancy laughed. "How could I forget?" She'd shown up at a country club dance, sure that no one else would be wearing a dress like hers because she'd ordered it from a fancy department store in New York. Five minutes later Laurie had walked in with Adam, her dress a carbon copy of Nancy's.

"I remember, all right," she said. "You and I have always had similar tastes. We liked the same guy in sixth grade—"

"We both got blue bicycles for Christmas that year, too," Laurie put in, her eyes twinkling.

"Now I've got a blue Mustang," Nancy said.

Laurie grinned. "Hey—I have a red one," she replied. "Guess you've still got good taste, Nan."

The music ended, and George and Bess returned. Bess sat down and tossed her long blonde hair over her shoulder, fanning her flushed cheeks. "I'm thirsty," she announced, signaling the waitress who had brought Jon's note to Laurie.

Pam returned, an unpleasant expression on her otherwise pretty face. She tapped the notepad in her hand. "What'll it be?" she asked, and though the words were directed at Bess, she was glaring at Laurie.

Bess, George, and Nancy ordered sodas. Laurie shook her head when Pam asked her. The waitress scowled.

Poor Laurie looked really uncomfortable. Trying to help her out, Nancy started chattering. "Hey, you guys, guess what? Laurie's got a Mustang, too."

George chuckled. "That's amazing, you two are still choosing the same things."

A few minutes later Pam returned with a tray of cold drinks. She set a soda down in front of each girl with a thud—until she got to Laurie. Then, with an odd little smile, she said, "Mr. Villiers said, 'With my compliments.'" She picked up a stemmed crystal goblet of soda.

"All right, Laurie! What a great guy," Nancy said, applauding. Bess and George joined in.

Just then Pam bumped the goblet with the edge of her hand. It tipped—right into Laurie's lap!

Laurie gave a stunned cry as the soda splattered over her jeans, T-shirt, and jean jacket.

"Oh, I'm terribly sorry!" Pam insisted, as she surveyed the damage she'd done. Nancy didn't miss the glint of pleasure shining in her eyes, though. She was sure the move had been deliberate.

"It's okay," Laurie said lamely, dabbing at her clothes with the paper napkins George had handed her. "I was going to leave soon anyway. I promised my parents I'd get home early."

Without giving anyone else a chance to speak, Pam hurried off. Nancy followed, on impulse, and saw Pam and Adam Boyd meet in front of the doors leading into the kitchen. As she watched, Adam handed Pam some money. Then they went their separate ways.

"I see you're still sticking your nose into everybody else's business," commented a familiar voice.

Nancy turned to see Brenda Carlton standing practically at her elbow. Brenda wrote articles for the River Heights newspaper and considered herself a star reporter. As far as Nancy was concerned, Brenda was more of a star nuisance.

"Nice to see you, too, Brenda," she said cheerfully, before returning to her table.

Laurie was about to leave, and Bess looked as if she'd had enough of Moves, too. "I'm exhausted from all that dancing! Let's go rent a movie or something," she said.

George and Nancy exchanged a look; they were ready to leave, too. "Sounds great to me," George said.

The four girls were moving toward the door when a male voice called out, "Laurie, wait!"

Jon had left the sound booth and was working his way through the crowd. Laurie hesitated. She looked from Nancy to George to Bess. "You haven't forgotten about my party tomorrow, have you?" she asked. "I'm really going all out."

"We'll be there," Nancy promised.

Bess and George nodded their agreement.

The three friends went outside, leaving Laurie behind to talk with Jon.

"He's so romantic. Too good to be true," Bess said with a sigh.

Nancy laughed. "You mustn't have been talking to Adam," she remarked. "The whole time we were dancing, he told me how rotten Jon is and how sorry Laurie's going to be if she gets too involved with him."

"Yeah, he tried that one on me, too," George put in.

A soft summer breeze ruffled Nancy's hair as

they walked across the parking lot toward her car. Suddenly George stopped dead and grabbed Nancy's arm. "Look," she cried.

Nancy followed George's pointing finger. She gasped out loud.

"Oh, no!" Bess groaned.

All four of the Mustang's tires had been slashed!

Chapter

Two

"Wʜᴀᴛ ᴛʜᴇ—" George began.

"Nancy, who could have done this?" Bess cried.

"Why is the question," Nancy murmured.

She stared at the slash marks for a moment, then sighed. She and George and Bess wouldn't be going anywhere until all the tires had been replaced. "Come on," she said grimly, heading back to the club. "Let's call a gas station."

Nancy found the pay phone and started flipping through the directory with George looking over her shoulder. Jon Villiers was just coming down the hall from his office, and Bess immediately struck up a conversation with him.

"It's awful," she said. "Just awful."

"What's awful?" Nancy heard him ask. She was dialing the number of a nearby service station.

"Nancy's tires were slashed," Bess answered. "I'm Bess Marvin," she went on as Nancy waited for someone to answer on the other end of the line. "These are my friends, Nancy Drew and George Fayne."

"Jon Villiers," the deejay introduced himself with a dazzling smile. Nancy could see now that his eyes were an intense shade of blue.

Jon glanced at his watch. "It's midnight. If you're trying to get a mechanic at this hour, you probably won't have much luck. Why don't you let me drive you home?"

Nancy looked at each of her friends to see how they felt about the situation. George shrugged her shoulders, and Bess was all smiles. Nancy nodded. "Thank you," she said.

"I'm sorry about your tires," Jon told Nancy when the four of them were settled in his car. "I feel sort of responsible—since I own Moves."

"Have you had any other vandalism?" Nancy asked.

Jon shook his head. There was a short pause, then he changed the subject. "You're friends of Laurie's, aren't you?"

"Yes," Nancy answered. "We went to school with her."

Again he hesitated, concentrating on the road. "I've only been going with her a couple of weeks, and I don't really know her family. What are they like?"

"Well, you know she's an only child," Bess replied from the back seat, where she and George were sitting.

Jon nodded. "Yes, I knew that. So I guess her parents have pretty much given her everything she wants," he went on.

The conversation was beginning to make Nancy feel uncomfortable. "Laurie isn't spoiled, if that's what you mean," she said.

"But her parents are wealthy," Bess put in.

George gave Bess a look. "I'd like to know who slashed Nancy's tires," George said, changing the subject. She seemed to feel the same way about Jon's questions as Nancy did.

"It was probably just a random thing," Jon said. "Kids, maybe. If you were Laurie, which would you rather get from a guy—flowers or candy?"

Nancy turned slightly, catching George's eye. She raised an eyebrow.

When the girls reached Nancy's house, they thanked Jon and went inside to report the incident to the police. "Let's skip the movie," Nancy suggested after hanging up the phone. "We've got too much to talk about."

Within a few minutes they had popped a batch of popcorn and were settled down in the den to talk.

"All right, you guys. Who could have been mad enough at me to do that to my tires?" Nancy asked, voicing the thought that had been going round and round in her mind.

George looked at Nancy and shook her head. "I don't know. Brenda Carlton, maybe?"

"Slashing tires isn't Brenda's style. No, I think —Hey!" Nancy snapped her fingers and sat up a little straighter. "What if the slashing was meant for someone else?"

Bess and George looked blank. "I'd swear that Adam paid that waitress to dump that soft drink on Laurie—I saw him giving her money afterward. Maybe he did the same thing with Laurie's tires—except Pam, or whomever he paid, got my car instead. They'd be easy to confuse in the dark."

George nodded. "He could have done it himself, for that matter. The club was so crowded, no one would notice people going in and out."

"Adam always seemed like such a nice guy," Bess said. "This break-up with Laurie has really changed him."

Nancy sighed. "I know," she said. "I know."

* * *

The service station attendant dusted his hands together as he stepped back from Nancy's car. He'd just replaced Nancy's tires with brand-new ones. "There you go," he said. "You're back in business."

Nancy gave him a check. "Thanks," she said, sliding behind the wheel as George and Bess climbed into the car.

"Let's head for the mall and just put the whole incident out of our minds for a while so we can concentrate on finding really great outfits to wear to Laurie's party," Bess said, brightening.

After they'd been shopping for about an hour, the girls ran into Laurie.

"Oh, hi! I'm just picking up some stuff for the party," Laurie said. She was loaded down with boutique bags.

"Are you giving away clothes as party favors?" Nancy asked.

Laurie laughed, blushing. "Well, I needed a few things myself," she admitted.

Nancy suggested they all stop for a soda.

Nancy gestured toward Laurie's shopping bag after they were seated with drinks. "Show us what you're going to wear today."

Looking pleased, Laurie pulled a sleek blue jersey dress from the bag and stood up to hold it against herself.

Nancy laughed. "I almost bought the same dress," she told Laurie.

"It's true." Bess was wide-eyed. "Nancy tried it on and everything."

Laurie seemed to have stars in her eyes. "I want to look especially nice for Jon," she said.

"He's really special to you, isn't he?" Nancy asked softly.

Laurie nodded. "I don't know what it is about him. I haven't even known him very long—only a couple of weeks. But he seems—well—right for me." She sighed. "My parents haven't said that much to me about him, but I can tell they're a little worried. He's older, he's not from here, no one knows anything about him—well, you know how parents worry. That's partly why I'm having the party. I know they'll like him once they really get a chance to know him."

Nancy looked thoughtfully at Laurie. Although he seemed nice, Jon Villiers was a stranger in River Heights. She hoped Laurie wasn't about to be hurt.

"Ned's coming to the party, too, isn't he?" Laurie asked, continuing.

Nancy nodded, her face slightly flushed. The thought of her boyfriend, Ned Nickerson, always made her glow and feel happy. "I called him this morning and left a message about it," she answered, smiling.

Nancy, Bess, and George continued shopping until they'd found a perfect outfit for Nancy—a white cotton blouse-and-skirt set with a wide black belt.

As Nancy was fumbling with her key in her front door, she heard the phone ring three times. Bursting into the front hall, she dropped her bags and ran to pick the phone up on the fifth ring. "Hello." It was Ned.

"I was just about to hang up. Short notice on that party, Drew," Ned said, pretending to grumble. "Still, I guess I can rearrange my incredibly heavy schedule for you. Should I pick you up or meet you there?"

"Nickerson, I appreciate your sacrifice, really I do," Nancy teased. "How about if I pick you up? I promised to give George and Bess a ride."

After agreeing on a time, Nancy told Ned about the slashed-tire episode at Moves.

Ned gave a long, low whistle. "Sounds like you're on somebody's list," he said, sounding worried. "Any idea whose?"

"I have one idea," Nancy replied, "but nothing really solid." She didn't want to mention her theory about Adam Boyd until she had more to go on. They talked a little longer, then Nancy hung up to get ready for the party.

At five o'clock sharp, Nancy, Ned, George, and Bess arrived at the Weavers' house, in the section of River Heights built exclusively of mansions.

The party had been set up on the lawn, and Nancy smiled when she saw young waiters in tuxedos and high-top sneakers solemnly handing around trays of hamburgers and hot dogs. Trust Laurie to do it in style.

"Wow," Bess said for all of them.

"It's like something out of a prime-time soap opera," George commented, obviously impressed. All the girls had been to parties at the Weavers' before, but this one was really special. Spectacular displays of cut flowers were set around the yard in giant urns. A yellow and white striped tent canopy rose up at the back of the lush one-acre lawn. A three-table buffet was set up to their right with damask tablecloths and huge silver candelabra.

Laurie popped out of the crowd. She looked radiant in the blue jersey dress Nancy had almost bought. After chatting a minute, Bess dragged George off to check out the buffet.

Nancy noticed that Laurie's attention was wandering. She kept looking toward the house, and Nancy guessed she must be watching for Jon.

Just then her waiting was rewarded. Jon moved through the crowd to greet Laurie with an eager smile and a kiss on the cheek. She introduced him to Ned, and the two young men shook hands.

"So, what do you think?" Nancy asked after Laurie had led Jon off to talk to her parents.

19

"About what?" Ned replied, playing dumb.

Nancy elbowed him lightly in the ribs. "About Jon Villiers," she answered.

Ned shrugged. "He isn't my type," he said with a laugh. "Let's go dance."

Under the canopy a wooden dance floor had been set up, and a band played rock from a large gazebo nearby.

"This really is some party," Ned observed.

Nancy nodded. Over Ned's shoulder, she saw Jon excuse himself and wander back to the house.

At the end of the next dance, Nancy went inside to brush her hair. Since the downstairs powder room was occupied, she went up to the second floor of the mansion, knowing the Weavers wouldn't mind.

As she was passing the closed door to Mr. Weaver's study, she heard Jon's voice. He was speaking loudly, obviously anxious about something. Nancy paused in the hallway. Maybe she could help.

What Jon said next stopped her from revealing her presence, however. "Look," he snarled, "I've got enough problems without making her suspicious. I've talked to her, and everything is fine—"

Nancy's eyes widened. Whose suspicions was Jon worried about? Who was he talking to?

Jon's voice sank in volume. After glancing up and down the hallway to make sure she wasn't being observed, Nancy pressed her ear directly against the door.

"I told you not to worry!" Jon burst out suddenly. "I'll take care of her."

Chapter

Three

Jon's words echoed in Nancy's mind as she hurried back down the stairs. "I told you not to worry!" he'd practically shouted. "I'll take care of her!"

The question was, who was he planning to "take care of," and how?

The rest of the party went by in a blur for Nancy. She kept an eye on Jon, but he didn't do anything unusual. What had his words meant? Could he have been talking about Laurie?

As she pulled into Ned's driveway to drop him off, Nancy thought of another possibility. What if Jon had been talking about her?

Nancy Drew, that's crazy, she scolded herself. But the thought stubbornly refused to go away. It was possible, after all. Nancy did have a reputation around River Heights—everyone knew she was a detective. If Jon was involved in some kind of shady dealings, he might decide he didn't want some curious private eye hanging around his club. It was just possible. . . .

"Hey! Earth to Nancy. Anybody home?" Ned was gently shaking Nancy's arm.

"Oh, sorry." Nancy blushed. "I guess I was just—thinking."

"So what else is new?" Ned asked with a grin. "You know, not to change the subject, but for some reason, I seem to be in love with you."

Nancy could feel her face widen into a grin. Ned, tall and handsome, always had this effect on her—he could make her feel ridiculously happy.

"I love you, too," she whispered, leaning forward. Their lips met in a long, melting kiss.

When they drew apart, Nancy felt a little dazed.

"What is on your mind, Drew?" Ned asked, stroking her cheek tenderly.

Nancy smiled. "Nothing," she said dreamily. "Nothing at all."

The next day, however, the questions returned to plague Nancy. She thought about Jon's words all day—through her errands, through lunch with her father, who was going out of town on business, through a game of tennis with George.

Could Jon Villiers have been the one who slashed her tires? And if he had, what was he planning next? How was he going to "take care of her"—if at all?

She was no closer to an answer when Ned came to pick her up that night.

"You look great," he said quietly as Nancy opened the front door to him.

Nancy smiled. "Thanks," she answered. "You look pretty good yourself."

Hannah Gruen, who had been the Drews' housekeeper since Nancy's mother had died fifteen years earlier, wandered into the living room. "Hello, Ned," she said warmly. "And where are you two off to this evening?"

"We're meeting Laurie Weaver and her friend Jon Villiers for dinner," Nancy told Hannah.

Hannah raised an eyebrow. "Isn't he the owner of that new dance club? The one where your tires were slashed? Nancy, are you getting involved in another mystery?"

Nancy smiled. "Could be."

When Nancy and Ned arrived at the restaurant where they'd agreed to meet the other couple, Laurie was already there, wearing a scoop-neck pink dress and white flats. But there was no sign of Jon among the other diners waiting to be seated.

Laurie looked anxiously at her elegant gold watch. "Do you suppose something's happened to Jon?" she fretted. "He should have been here by now."

Nancy gave her friend a reassuring smile as they were seated. "I'm sure he'll be along in a few minutes," she said.

Twenty more minutes passed and still no Jon. Nancy noticed that Laurie couldn't keep her mind on the conversation; she kept glancing out the window. Every time a car pulled into the parking lot, Laurie peered out to see if it was Jon's.

A full forty-five minutes had gone by when Jon finally did arrive. His smile was warm and apologetic.

"I'm sorry," he told Laurie earnestly, taking one of her hands in his. "I tried a shortcut along the old river road and ended up with a flat tire. It took me a long time to put on the spare."

Nancy looked at Jon's spotless pale yellow shirt, white jeans, and clean hands and knew in an instant that he was lying; a glance in Ned's direction told her that he was thinking the same thing.

"Well," Ned said, trying to smooth over the uneasy moment. "Let's eat. I'm starved."

Dinner was pleasant, but after only a few minutes, Nancy began to feel as if she and Ned were intruding. Jon was interested only in Laurie. He spent most of the meal staring dreamily into her eyes and hardly touching his food. Laurie seemed almost as smitten as he was. Nancy and Ned ended up talking to each other, and when they said good night to Laurie and Jon, the two love-birds barely noticed their departure.

"There sure seem to be a lot of flat tires going around," Ned said after they were buckled into his car.

"I know what you mean," Nancy agreed, thinking of her slashed tires and of the flat that had supposedly delayed Jon that evening. "In my opinion, it's almost impossible to change a tire in white jeans without getting dirty."

"No smudges of grease on his hands, either. Did you notice that?"

Nancy nodded. "But he could have stopped someplace to wash up," she said.

"He could have changed his clothes, too, I suppose," Ned suggested. "But it doesn't seem very likely that he brought extra jeans along, just in case he had a flat tire." He started the car finally. "One thing is obvious. He's crazy about Laurie."

"And Laurie's crazy about him," Nancy agreed. She was gazing out at the stars, worrying about her friend.

Nancy drew a deep breath and exhaled. "I think it's possible that Jon was the one who slashed my tires," she confided.

Ned tossed her a look of surprise before turning his attention back to the road. "What?" he demanded.

"I didn't mention it to you because I wanted to think about the whole thing first, but yesterday at Laurie's party I overheard Jon talking on the telephone." She paused. "He was telling someone not to worry, that he'd 'take care of her.'"

"And you think you might be the 'her' he was referring to?"

Nancy hesitated before answering. "I'm not sure, but it seems possible, doesn't it?"

Ned thought for a moment. "I guess. Except the tire slashing happened before the phone call."

Nancy looked out the window. "There was something about his tone, about the conversation itself. I can't tell you how I know, but I could tell it wasn't the first time Jon had said those things, Ned."

The expression on Ned's face was serious. "What do you mean?" he asked.

She shrugged. "He sounded as if he'd been over the same ground before." Nancy sighed. "And I can't rule Adam Boyd out, either," Nancy continued.

"What?" Ned asked, and Nancy told him

about her other suspect. "This is getting complicated," he said.

"Want to come in for a while?" Nancy asked when they pulled into her driveway.

Ned gave her a quick kiss and shook his head. "Sorry. I promised Dad I'd watch the baseball game with him if he taped it. Don't forget I'm going fishing with him tomorrow. Can you manage without me?"

"I won't enjoy it, but I will bumble through," Nancy promised.

Ned got out of the car and walked Nancy to her porch. There, in front of the door, he kissed her again. She was still feeling a little flushed when she went into the house and wandered out to the kitchen.

Hannah was puttering around in her bathrobe. "Did you have a nice time?" she asked.

Nancy smiled and nodded, setting her purse on the table.

Hannah yawned. "Well, I'm off to bed. I know it's early, but I'm exhausted."

"See you in the morning, Hannah," Nancy said, kissing her good night.

The telephone rang just as Nancy was leaving the kitchen. She answered it quickly. "Drew residence."

Someone was sobbing quietly on the other end of the line. "Nancy? Is that you?"

"Who is this?" Nancy asked, alarmed. Suddenly she was wide awake.

"It's m-me—Laurie," her friend stammered. "Oh, Nancy, you've got to come over here, quick!"

"Laurie, calm down and tell me what's the matter," Nancy said evenly.

Laurie began to cry again. "Oh Nancy, I'm so scared—my parents aren't home, and the servants are out—oh, please, Nan, come over right away!"

"I'll be there in five minutes," she promised. She hung up the phone and hurried out the back door. Moments later she was backing down the driveway and turning on the street toward the Weavers'.

Laurie met her at the curb. "I found this hanging from the front door when I got home from my date with Jon," she told Nancy, holding out a piece of rope.

Nancy reached for it, then began to shiver. What Laurie had handed her wasn't just a piece of rope. It had a single loop with thirteen twists around it—a hangman's noose!

Chapter

Four

NANCY FELT A CHILL race down her spine as she turned the noose over in her hands to examine it in the porch light. She looked at Laurie. "Obviously you didn't see anybody, but was there a note or anything?"

Laurie's lower lip quivered when she answered, "There was a note. Come into my mom's study and I'll show you."

The note wasn't much of a lead. It was written in bold black letters on a page torn from a ledger. "For pretty Laurie with my compliments," it read.

Putting down the note, Nancy recalled where

she had heard "with my compliments" before. That was it. Jon. Jon had told the waitress to use those exact words when he sent Laurie the soda at Moves the other night. Did that mean Jon had sent this note? It would explain why he had been late for dinner, too.

On the other hand, there was the strong possibility that Adam Boyd had arranged the soda incident. And the tire slashing.

Nancy sighed. Only one thing was certain—someone was out to scare Laurie. But why?

"What are you thinking?" Laurie asked, a slight quaver in her voice.

Nancy gave her friend a reassuring smile and put an arm around her shoulders. "Everything's going to be all right," she promised. But she was worried.

"Was Jon with you when you got home?" Nancy asked.

Laurie shook her head. "I drove to the restaurant in my own car. Jon had to go back to Moves but he offered to take me home. I told him I'd be okay by myself." She glanced at the noose, lying where Nancy had put it on Mrs. Weaver's writing desk. "Now I wish he'd been here," she added in a quiet, distracted voice.

Nancy hesitated. "What about Adam?" she asked after a long time. "Do you think he'd be capable of something like this?"

Laurie went pale. She shrugged. "I don't know.

He was upset when I broke up with him, and he'd made it clear that he doesn't like Jon."

Nancy sighed. "I didn't mention this before because I didn't want to worry you unnecessarily, but I saw Adam giving our waitress, Pam, money just after she spilled that soda all over you."

Laurie's eyes widened. "You think he paid her to do that?"

"That's the way it looks." Nancy paused. "I'm afraid there's more. Laurie, I think—especially after tonight—that whoever slashed my tires was really out to get you, not me."

"You mean someone got confused because our cars are so similar?" Laurie guessed. Nancy nodded.

"I thought I knew Adam," Laurie went on sadly. "I mean, sure he was hurt when we broke up, but I never would have believed he'd do anything so mean."

"Maybe it wasn't Adam," Nancy reflected. She watched Laurie closely for a reaction. "Maybe it was Jon."

"Nancy! He'd never do any of these things. Anyway, he couldn't have," Laurie protested, looking angry now. "He was at dinner with us, and then at the movie—"

"And he was forty-five minutes late," Nancy pointed out gently. "He could have come over here and left the noose before meeting us at the restaurant."

Laurie shook her head wildly. "No," she insisted. "He had a flat tire. Why are you saying these things? Jon loves me!"

Nancy knew now wasn't the time to tell Laurie what she'd overheard Jon saying at the party. Instead, Nancy touched her friend's arm. "Try to calm down," she urged Laurie. "You don't want to be upset when the police get here."

"The police?" Laurie whispered, horrified. "I don't want them involved in this!"

Nancy lifted the noose from Mrs. Weaver's desk. "Laurie, when your parents get home and see this, they'll call the police anyway."

Laurie snatched the noose from Nancy's hand, carried it over to the fireplace and tossed it onto the grate. She piled wadded-up newspapers on top and reached for a match.

"Laurie, that's important evidence," Nancy warned.

Laurie didn't seem to hear. She adjusted the flue, then set the newspaper on fire. After a moment she rose to her feet and turned to face Nancy. "I'm begging you, Nancy—don't say anything about this to my parents."

"Why not?" Nancy wanted to know.

Laurie's expression was troubled. Nancy knew there was something her friend was keeping from her. "I just don't want them to know, that's all. If you really care about me, Nancy, you won't say anything."

Nancy wanted to find out what Laurie was hiding, but she knew it would be useless to try that night. Instead, she asked Laurie for a flashlight, and the two of them went outside and circled the house to look for clues. Nancy was hoping to find tracks in the flowerbeds or the lawn, or something that the intruder might have dropped, but there was nothing.

She and Laurie were just completing the search when the Weavers came home.

"Who's there?" Mr. Weaver immediately called out, seeing the flashlight.

"It's only us, Daddy," Laurie called. "Nancy lost one of her earrings at the party yesterday afternoon, and we were hoping to find it."

Mrs. Weaver's voice was warm and full of concern. "Surely you'd have a better chance of finding the earring in the daylight," she suggested.

"We thought maybe it would catch the light," Laurie answered.

Nancy was amazed at the web of lies her friend had woven in the space of a minute or so, but she didn't say anything. If Laurie wanted to keep secrets from her parents, Nancy wouldn't stop her—yet. But she did want to find out why Laurie insisted on being so secretive.

Laurie followed Nancy to her car. That haunted expression was still in Laurie's eyes, and

Nancy couldn't resist asking, "What is it that you're not telling me?"

Laurie sighed miserably. "Jon didn't leave the club to meet us when he said he did," she confessed. "I know, because I called him before you and Ned got there and Pam told me he'd already been gone for a long time."

So Jon could have come to Laurie's house and put the noose in place, along with the note. Nancy was positive he'd lied about his flat tire. He was looking more suspicious by the minute.

Nancy sighed. "Be careful," she said, slipping her key into the ignition.

Laurie's smile was sudden and filled with confidence. "I've got Nancy Drew, famous detective, on my side," she said. "What do I have to worry about?"

"Be careful, anyway," Nancy said, before starting the engine and driving away.

The next afternoon, after spending the morning at the country club, Nancy decided to pay an unexpected visit to Moves to investigate Jon Villiers.

Nancy sat in the parking lot at Moves for a few minutes, looking at the long, low building and thinking. There were no other cars there except for Jon's and an old convertible with a dented fender. What was she going to say to Jon Villiers, anyway? What exactly was she hoping to find out? She didn't know, but the trouble had begun at Moves, so the investigation might as well start there, too.

Nancy tried the club's front door. Locked. She went around the side and tried another door. Locked again.

At the back of the club, Nancy found the delivery entrance open and stepped into an empty kitchen.

"Hello?" she called, though not very loudly.

She heard music in the distance, soft and romantic.

"Hello?" she said again, crossing the kitchen and entering a long hallway. The music was louder now, and Nancy recognized the tune. It was a love song.

To Nancy's right was a short hallway with a frosted glass door marked Office. She knocked. There was no answer, so she tried the knob. It gave and Nancy peeked inside, but before she could investigate, the music stopped. She was alert in the sudden silence, listening for a voice or an approaching footstep.

When the same love song started playing all over again, she decided to check out who was playing the music. Nancy moved quietly down the hallway and inched open the door leading into the main part of the club, not sure that she wanted to be seen.

Black lights blazed, making the white checkers on the floor glow eerily. The TV monitors all showed a strange, shifting pattern of colored light. Music rolled from the giant speakers, soft and sad.

In the center of the floor, Jon and Pam moved together in a slow dance, their movements smooth and practiced. It occurred to Nancy that they must have danced together many times before. Her mind raced through the possibilities as she stood looking on, unseen, from the doorway.

Pam looked up at Jon and laid one hand tenderly against his face. He stared down at her for a long time, then slowly, deliberately backed up away from her. "It's over," he said. "We have to forget the past."

Nancy could feel Pam's rage, even from a distance. The girl glared up at Jon for a long moment, then whirled away, her movements sharp and defiant. "There's one thing I'm never going to forget, Jon Villiers," she spat out. "I'm never going to forget what a criminal you are!"

Chapter

Five

HIS EXPRESSION UNREADABLE, Jon turned on his heel and strode toward the doorway where Nancy was standing. She eased the door closed and barely had time to duck into a supply closet. Jon went into his office and slammed the door.

Nancy sneaked out through the kitchen and to the safety of her car. She didn't want to confront Jon and Pam about what she'd heard until she'd had time to piece it together.

She drove off, the wheels in her mind turning as fast as her tires. What if Pam acted on her anger? Could Laurie be in danger?

By the time Nancy reached George's house the

only thing she'd decided was to investigate Jon Villiers's background.

George met her at the front door, looking none the worst for the morning she had spent at the dentist's office. "What's happening?" George asked immediately.

Nancy told her everything that had happened that morning.

"What now?" George asked.

"We've got to do some serious investigation," Nancy answered. "I have a plan, and I need you guys to distract Jon for me tonight. After we've picked Bess up, I'll tell you the details."

Jon Villiers was in the sound booth that evening. "He looks as terrific as ever," Bess said. And Nancy wondered if there really could be a crook lurking behind that handsome face.

George and Bess sidled through the crowd to a table near the booth as Nancy watched. She smiled. No one would think they were out to do anything but have a good time, the way they talked and laughed with everyone around them. But Nancy knew they were ready to stop Jon if he left the booth and keep him distracted until she gave them the all-clear signal.

She waited until a new dance began before starting toward the back of the club, where Jon's office was. Nancy checked to make sure there was no one in the long hallway to the kitchen. No waiters or waitresses around. She tore down the hall and into the short hallway where Jon's office was located.

The squeak of sneakers on linoleum flattened her against the wall. A tall, gangly waiter with a shock of blond hair staggered by, beneath a giant tray, followed by Pam.

Once the area was quiet again, Nancy turned the doorknob to Jon's office. It was locked, but Nancy opened it quickly with a credit card. She slipped inside and stood perfectly still until her eyes adjusted and she was able to see by the dim light coming in through the window behind Jon's desk.

Nancy made her way across the room and pulled a tiny penlight from her pocket. All the time she was flipping through the papers on Jon's desk, she listened. If someone found her in this room, in the dark, no excuse in the world would be good enough to get her off the hook.

After five minutes of searching, Nancy found a bank statement and a stack of cancelled checks. There were four different ones, made out for large amounts, all to the same man. Flipping them over, Nancy saw that they'd been cashed at a Chicago bank—

In the same instant Nancy's heart practically stopped. There were voices in the hall.

She flicked off the penlight and crouched down behind the desk. The only other way out was through the window, and she listened to the people outside the door as she slowly eased the window up.

"I really care about you, Laurie, you know that," Jon was saying, "but I don't think we should see each other anymore—at least not for a while."

Nancy could hear tears in Laurie's voice when she answered. "You can't do this. I broke up with Adam for you—you mean everything to me!"

Jon sounded sad, but reasonable. And much nearer. Nancy lunged out the open window only an instant before she heard Jon's key in the lock.

"I'm not good enough for you," Nancy heard him say.

Nancy, who was standing outside, with her back to the wall, heard Laurie cry, "Don't say things like that! The past is over!"

"How did that window get open?" Jon muttered.

Nancy knew he was about to look out the window, so she didn't hang around to hear more. She scurried off into the shadows.

After a few minutes she wandered back inside the club and took a seat at George and Bess's table. Pam was standing nearby, and Nancy felt as if she had been watching her.

"Thanks a lot for keeping Jon occupied," she muttered. "He almost caught me."

"We tried," Bess insisted. "But once he saw

Laurie, there was no keeping him away. Did you find out anything?"

Nancy looked around. She saw Brenda Carlton sitting at a table nearby. Her old rival smiled a syrupy smile and waggled three fingers in greeting. Everything about her said, "I know you're up to something, Nancy Drew."

"I don't want to talk about it here," she said. "Let's go."

"But I didn't get to dance yet," Bess complained.

"All right," Nancy agreed with a smile. "Go ahead and dance."

"There's Laurie," George said, looking across the crowded club. "She looks upset."

"Maybe we'd better go and talk to her," Nancy said. She already knew what the problem was, but she'd have to wait to explain it to George.

Pam pushed past Nancy with a tray full of sodas just as she and George reached Laurie. She stopped to serve the drinks at a nearby table, but she was frowning at Laurie with an expression of real dislike.

"Are you okay?" George asked Laurie, touching her arm.

Laurie's face was streaked with tears, but she smiled and said, "Sure. I'm fine. Why wouldn't I be?" With that, she turned and hurried off.

Out of the corner of her eye, Nancy saw Pam glance curiously in her direction, but she paid no attention. Laurie was leaving. Nancy followed her to the parking lot.

"Why don't you wait and go out for a bite with us?" Nancy asked her friend.

Laurie shook her head. "I need to be alone," she said, looking and sounding calmer than before. "You can do one thing for me, though. Stop your investigation. I don't want anything to upset Jon. I've got to keep him, Nancy."

There was nothing Nancy could do but watch Laurie drive away. She turned and went back inside to wait for Bess and George.

Hannah was vacuuming the living room the next morning when Nancy went into her father's study. She closed the door and flipped through his phone directory until she found the number of a contact named Mack Simpson. Mack was a detective on the Chicago police force.

He was delighted to hear from Nancy. "On a new case, are you?" he teased. "Well, I hope you're being careful."

"I am," Nancy assured him. "I need some information, Mack, and I was wondering if you could help."

"For Carson Drew's daughter, anything," Mack replied. "What do you need?"

Nancy gave him Jon Villiers's name. "I want to know if this man's ever been in any serious trouble with the police," she said. "He's involved with a friend of mine, and—well—some suspicious things have been happening lately."

"No problem," Mack answered. "I'll get back to you as soon as I've run this guy through the computer."

Fifteen minutes later, Mack called back. Jon Villiers had a prior record—a conviction for burglary two years earlier. And there was something else—he'd been charged with assaulting a police officer! Nancy called George and then Bess and arranged to meet them at the pizza place in the mall. She wanted to discuss this news in person.

"Well?" Bess demanded, when they were all together.

"What's happened?" George asked, a breath after Bess had spoken.

"I told you last night about finding the checks made out to a man in Chicago," Nancy said. "Well, today I called the police department there and they ran a make on Jon Villiers for me. He's got a prior record for burglary—and he assaulted a police officer."

Bess was round-eyed. "That does it. Jon is a crook. Maybe he's setting Laurie's folks up for a kidnapping or something. We've got to warn Laurie right away!"

Nancy sighed, remembering how torn up Laurie had sounded the night before, when Jon had told her they shouldn't see each other anymore.

"I'm not sure what's going on," she said. "From what I heard last night, Jon wants to break off the relationship. Maybe he really does want what's best for Laurie."

"What do you think, George?" Bess asked her cousin.

George's expression was serious. "I think Nancy's right. Granted, it doesn't look good, Jon's having a police record and all, but lots of people make a mistake when they're young and then straighten out later on."

Nancy nodded. "Besides, it's also obvious from what I heard Laurie say to Jon last night that she knows something about his past already."

Then she went on. "There are a lot of pieces that don't fit together, though. Why is Jon trying to break off with Laurie all of a sudden, when anybody could see he's still crazy about her? And what does the noose left on Laurie's porch have to do with all this?"

Bess only shrugged and ordered another soda.

"It's possible that we've got two games going on here, instead of just one," Nancy continued. "Maybe Adam and Jon are both involved, in different ways and for different reasons."

"I say we figure this out at the lake," Bess said.

"It's summer, and as long as we're just going to be thinking, let's do it someplace fun."

Nancy and George agreed, and when Nancy got home to pick up her suit, she noticed the message light on her answering machine blinking. She pushed the button to rewind it and called Ned to ask him to meet them at the lake.

After she hung up, she turned the machine on and stiffened at the message and voice. "You're dancing with danger, Nancy Drew," a horribly distorted, grating voice warned. "You'd better stop snooping where you don't belong."

Nancy played the message again, listening carefully, but she still didn't recognize the voice. It sounded mechanical.

Well, if someone thinks a telephone threat is going to stop me, he or she is wrong, Nancy reflected. But as she changed into her bathing suit, she had to admit that the case was turning into something much bigger—and much scarier —than a simple act of vandalism. And she had to find out who was behind it all—before it was too late.

Nancy told George and Bess about the call the minute she'd picked them up at Bess's house.

"You've got to tell the police the whole story," Bess told Nancy. "First the slashed tires and now a threatening message on your answering machine. Not to mention Laurie's noose. This is getting dangerous, Nan."

Nancy thought over what Bess had said while they picked their way through the crowd on the beach. Ned wasn't there yet, but Nancy did spot Laurie. Apparently she and Jon had ironed out their differences, because they were together. She recognized several of the waitresses from Moves, including Pam. Adam Boyd was hovering off to the side, watching Laurie and Jon with a venomous expression on his face.

Bess and George had stopped to greet friends, but Nancy, anxious to dive in, took off by herself. She dove from a pier and cut through the water in a sleek dive. She started to pull herself back to the surface with strong strokes.

But just as she should have reached the top, Nancy felt strong fingers grip her ankles and draw her back down to the bottom.

For a moment Nancy was too startled to be scared. Then as she was dragged deeper, her lungs began to burn with the need for oxygen. She tried to see her attacker, but the water was too murky, and she could make out nothing more than a slim, quick-moving shadow beneath her.

Nancy kicked hard, but couldn't free herself. Her mouth and nose were filling with water. She flailed her arms in an effort to reach the surface. No use.

She was going to drown!

Chapter

Six

WITH HER LAST BREATH, Nancy folded over into a sharp jackknife to reach down to try to break the grip on her ankles. Just then whoever had been grasping her ankles let go. And just as suddenly solid hands grabbed her waist and propelled her to the surface.

Sunlight and air rushed at Nancy when her head broke the surface of the water. Gasping and choking, she found herself looking into Ned's eyes.

"Somebody—somebody was pulling me down—" Nancy choked out the words.

48

After Ned helped her back onto the pier, she lay panting to catch her breath.

Out of the corner of her eye, Nancy saw Jon walking out of the lake, and down farther Adam Boyd. Either of them, or any of dozens of swimmers, could have been her attacker.

Seeing that Nancy would be all right, Ned said, "I've got to watch you every minute." Nancy wasn't fooled by his teasing tone. He'd been almost as scared as she was. "Turn my back on you for a day and what do you do? You almost drown."

Nancy laughed and kissed him, glad to be alive, glad that Ned was with her. She still felt a little shaky. "Thanks for the help, Nickerson," she retorted with a forced grin. "You have this great habit of showing up just in the nick of time."

They walked on the pier back to the beach, where Nancy spread her towel on the sand and lay back to let the sun warm her. Ned found his towel and joined her.

"What happened out there?" he asked in a quiet voice. There were lots of people around but none close enough to overhear.

Nancy drew in a deep breath—even now, she felt she needed extra air. "All I know is that someone must have been right behind me when I dove in. Before I could break the surface, he'd grabbed my ankles and pulled me down to the bottom."

"You didn't see anything?"

She shook her head. "Too murky. What about you—how did you happen to rescue me?"

Ned touched the back of her neck in a tender gesture. "I got to the lake in time to see you go in, and when you didn't come up when you should have, I got worried. There was no one behind you, Nan. He must have been waiting just under the surface."

"You didn't see him when you were down there, either?" Nancy asked.

"Only a flutter of legs and churning water as he swam away. Whoever it was probably had decided to let you go just then. After all, he had to be needing air as much as you."

Nancy nodded her agreement. She'd had a good scare, but now she began to think the incident might have only been a warning. She let out a long breath. "I suppose it was the same person who left the message on the answering machine."

Ned cupped his hand under Nancy's chin. "What message?" he asked, frowning.

Nancy told him about the telephone threat.

"The voice wasn't at all familiar? Was it male? Female?"

Nancy sighed. "I couldn't tell—it sounded

mechanical. It could have been a woman, I guess. It was pretty distorted."

"This is getting really nasty," Ned said.

Nancy agreed. But for Laurie's sake, as well as her own, she had to find out what was happening and who was behind it all.

"You'll be careful, won't you, Nan?" Ned asked, his eyes troubled. "I suppose you wouldn't give up the case—even if I said 'pretty please.'"

Nancy smiled. "I'll be very careful" was all she'd promise. She was already planning the next phase of her investigation.

Several hours later, after telling Ned she was going home to rest, Nancy showered and changed into dressy black pants, a tuxedo-style white shirt, and wide dark green belt. She looked up the number of Moves and dialed it from the phone in her bedroom after her hair was done. She and George and Bess had cooked up a plan on their way home from the lake.

"Moves," a masculine voice answered. "This is Jon."

"Jon, this is Nancy—Nancy Drew."

He sounded surprised. "Nancy, hi. What can I do for you?"

"The other night at dinner, you mentioned you were shorthanded at the club," she said.

"I could use a few more waitresses," he agreed. Now there was real curiosity in his voice. "Why?"

Nancy turned the phone cord around her index finger. "I'm looking for a job, Jon. How about giving me a chance to wait tables at Moves?"

He was silent. Nancy jumped in again before Jon could draw too many conclusions. "I want to buy my dad a birthday present," she said in an earnest voice. "And it's important to me to use my own money."

"Have you had any experience?" Jon wanted to know.

Nancy rolled her eyes, but her voice held a sweet note. "Of course I have," she said.

Jon hesitated for a second, then said, "Okay, Nancy. Come in tonight at seven. Pam will show you the ropes."

"Thanks, Jon," Nancy said. "You've done me a bigger favor than you know, she added to herself.

Pam met Nancy just after she went through the front door of Moves that night. Although she kept giving Nancy suspicious looks, she did help her find an apron and a Moves T-shirt. She went over the menu with her until Nancy knew the prices by heart.

"I think this is crazy," Bess whispered to Nancy when she and George came in later.

Nancy grinned at her friend, tapping her order pad with the end of her pencil. "I don't have time to stand around chit-chatting with the customers," she said in a mock-tough voice. "What'll it be?"

George laughed. "You've got this waitress act down," she said. "I'll have a cola."

"Me, too," Bess said, getting into the spirit.

Nancy was busy for the next two hours. At this rate, she thought, I'm never going to get any investigating done.

Just before her break, Brenda Carlton came in and deliberately sat in Nancy's section of the club. "Who do you think you're fooling with this waitress routine?" she asked.

Nancy favored her rival with a frosty smile. "How can I help you?" she countered, ignoring Brenda's question.

Brenda sighed. "You're up to something," she persisted. "What is it?"

Nancy widened her eyes. "Up to something? Why, I'm just doing my job, Brenda."

"Oh, brother," said Brenda, turning away.

Nancy smiled to herself and headed into the kitchen to take a break. The cooks were trying frantically to keep up with the orders.

"Have you worked here since the club opened?" Nancy asked one of the women, who was busy at the grill.

She didn't spare Nancy so much as a glance, though her voice wasn't unfriendly. "Yes," she said. "And there's been a time or two when I wished I hadn't even seen that ad in the paper."

"How well do you know our boss—Mr. Villiers?"

The woman looked Nancy over. She must have decided to trust her, for she answered, "I know he's young, and that he doesn't have much experience running a club."

Nancy didn't comment right then, since Pam showed up to leave a new order and pick up several others.

"I hear Jon's from Chicago," Nancy ventured when she and the grill girl were alone again.

The woman nodded. "I think so. He's got an uncle from there who comes to see him sometimes. They argue a lot, but I guess that's the way with family."

Nancy glanced at the clock on the kitchen wall. Her break had passed too quickly, but it hadn't been a waste of time. Could Jon's uncle be the man he'd been sending those big checks to, in Chicago? "Thanks for the company," she said, climbing down off the stool.

The cook smiled at her and nodded.

As Nancy left the kitchen, she practically collided with Adam Boyd. He took in her apron and T-shirt and acted annoyed.

"I heard you were working here," he said, his brow crinkled in a frown. "You wouldn't be here on a case, would you?"

Nancy knew he wouldn't believe her answer, but she wasn't about to admit that she was checking on Jon Villiers. "No," she answered. "I just want to pick up some extra cash."

Adam looked skeptical. "You? Why?"

"My dad's birthday is coming up," Nancy replied, making her way around him.

Nancy had been back at work for about half an hour when Laurie arrived and went immediately to the sound booth to talk with Jon, who took a break then. Jon and Laurie went out on the floor and danced, holding each other close, their gazes locked.

Nancy was caught by surprise when Jon and Laurie moved directly toward her. Laurie's arm was linked with Jon's, but her eyes were fixed on Nancy. She looked angry.

"You're working here?" she yelled, over the noise of the crowd, her gaze shifting from Nancy to Jon.

"She started tonight," Jon answered, looking pleased. Apparently he hadn't noticed how annoyed Laurie was.

Laurie's grip on Jon's arm tightened. She gave Nancy a cold look. Laurie knew Nancy was there to snoop and Laurie had asked Nancy to stop. Nancy watched her drag Jon off in the direction of his office.

It looked as if Nancy's days on the case were numbered.

Chapter

Seven

NANCY WAITED, expecting the ax to fall at any moment. Laurie would surely tell Jon about Nancy's reputation as an amateur detective. He would guess then why she'd wanted to work at Moves and fire her immediately.

But nothing happened. Jon came out of his office and went back to the sound booth without even glancing at Nancy.

Nancy didn't have time to think about what might be going on. The club was crowded, and she had to work hard until quitting time. Bess and George were waiting to ride home with her, and she told them about Laurie's reaction to seeing her working at the club.

"She's probably going to blow your cover," Bess said.

"Maybe not," George argued. "After all, if she was going to tell Jon about you, wouldn't she have done it by now?"

Nancy hoped George was right.

The next morning Nancy called Laurie at home. Mrs. Weaver answered and said her daughter had already left the house to meet a friend.

"Will you ask her to call me when she gets back, please?" Nancy asked.

After thanking Mrs. Weaver and hanging up, Nancy took her shower and dressed. As she was eating breakfast, the telephone rang. Nancy reached for it eagerly, hoping the caller was Laurie.

The voice on the other end of the line belonged to Ned. "Hello, Drew," he said. "How are you?"

Nancy answered with a smile in her words. "Well, nobody's tried to kill me today, if that's what you mean."

Ned chuckled. "And it's almost nine-thirty. So how's the case going? Have you found out anything new?"

"I haven't made any earth-shattering discoveries. But I did take a job at Moves," she admitted.

57

"Clever," Ned said, laughing. "You get rid of me so you can sneak out and get a job."

"Sorry," Nancy answered. "But it's really necessary for me to work there—the case is centered there. I know it. But I don't think Laurie wants to know if Jon's really up to something."

"Have you talked to her?"

"I tried," Nancy answered, "but she isn't home. I asked Mrs. Weaver to have her call me when she gets back."

"Maybe Laurie will keep your secret," Ned speculated. "Maybe she figures Jon doesn't have anything to hide."

"I wish that were true," Nancy said.

"How about going out to lunch with me?" Ned asked, changing the subject. "I could use a break from the insurance business."

Nancy chuckled. "You could apply for a job at Moves," she suggested.

"Let's talk about it over lunch," Ned came back good-naturedly. "I'll pick you up in three hours."

He arrived at Nancy's house with a picnic basket in the back of his car. They drove to the park and spent a happy afternoon laughing and talking together. By the time Ned brought her home again, Nancy felt refreshed.

After unsuccessfully trying Laurie again, Nancy showered, changed her clothes, and drove to

Moves for her six-o'clock shift. Pam Hastings met her just inside the club.

There was an unpleasant gleam in Pam's eyes. "Jon wants to see you in his office immediately," she said.

This is it, Nancy thought. As of right now, no more sleuthing.

When she knocked at the door of Jon's office, it was Laurie's voice that called out a weary "Come in."

Nancy entered, braced for an explosion, but Jon only looked up from the stack of papers he was going through and smiled.

"I'd like you to do me a favor, if you would," he said, handing over a set of keys.

Not knowing what else to do, Nancy accepted them. She tried to catch Laurie's eye, but Laurie wouldn't look at her.

Nancy turned her attention back to Jon. "What do you want me to do?"

"I'd like you to run over to my place and pick up some papers—"

"I could do that," Laurie broke in, giving Nancy a defiant look.

"I know," Jon said patiently. "But I have some friends coming in a few minutes, and I want you to meet them."

Although Laurie looked reluctant, she didn't say anything else, and Jon turned his attention back to Nancy. "I can spare you because you're still new," he explained. "And I really need these papers. The only time I could arrange a meeting with my accountant was after the club closes." He paused to glance at his watch. "I live at six fourteen Sycamore Street, number forty-eight. They should be in the top drawer of my desk, in a brown manila envelope."

Nancy's heart was beating a touch faster than usual. Jon didn't know it, but he was actually inviting her to search his apartment. She glanced at Laurie to see if she'd stop her.

When Laurie didn't say anything, Nancy turned and walked out the door.

She paused in the hallway, just out of sight, and listened as Laurie said, "Why do you trust Nancy when you hardly know her?"

Nancy held her breath, waiting for the answer.

It came quickly. "I have no reason not to trust her, do I?" he asked in a mild voice.

Laurie deliberated for what seemed an eternity to Nancy. "I guess not," she finally said.

Nancy silently thanked her friend for not giving her away and hurried out to the parking lot. Jon could be suspicious if she was gone too long.

The building was modest and ordinary, a brick structure probably twenty or thirty years old. Nancy was a little surprised—somehow she had expected Jon to live someplace more glamorous.

Wasting no time, she took the elevator to the fourth floor, and apartment number 48. She let herself in with Jon's key.

Nancy looked quickly around the living room, which seemed only partially furnished. There were no pictures on the walls, no books, no mementoes on the mantel above the fireplace. The couch looked as though it might have come from a cheap rental place or a thrift shop. There was nothing personal about the apartment—it might have been a shabby hotel room, rather than someone's home.

After glancing into the kitchen, Nancy walked into Jon's bedroom, which doubled as an office. An old easy chair, an army surplus desk, and a dented file cabinet sat clustered to one side of the room. The effect was bleak.

Nancy found Jon's manila envelope right off. She looked inside, but as she had guessed, it contained nothing more than receipts and register tapes from Moves. She was looking for something more. She went quickly and skillfully through the other papers on the desk.

After about five minutes of methodical searching, Nancy located a half-finished letter.

Dear Uncle Mike,

Everybody reaches a place in their life where they need a second chance. If you won't help me convince your friends to give me just a little more time, I don't know what I'm going to do. You're the only one I can count on.

There, the letter ended.

Nancy put it back in the exact position she'd found it and continued with her search. Her mind was trying to piece together what she'd learned. From the tone of that letter, Nancy guessed that Jon owed some men money, and that he was afraid of what they might do if he didn't pay them promptly.

Nancy went back to her work. In the bottom of the file cabinet, tucked away in the back, she found a package of pink envelopes that smelled vaguely of perfume.

Kneeling, Nancy removed the rubber band that bound them together and pulled out a letter.

It was a long and flowery expression of love, filled with dreams of an upcoming marriage. It was signed, "All my love forever, Sheila."

"Sheila," Nancy mused aloud. She hadn't heard Jon or anyone mention that name. She skimmed a few more letters and noticed that there was a two-year gap between a couple of them. Apparently, there had been a lapse in Sheila's devotion.

The telephone rang, startling Nancy. She put

the letters back in their hiding place, in the same order, wrapped in the same rubber band. Before she could decide whether or not to answer the phone, the ringing stopped. An answering machine had come on, and Jon's recorded voice filled the room.

There was a beep before she heard him say, "Nancy? If you're still there, will you please get on the phone?"

Nancy drew a deep breath and reached out for the receiver. "Hello, Jon," she said, trying to keep her voice light. Inside, she felt shaken as though she'd been caught.

"Hi," Jon said. He didn't sound angry or even the least bit suspicious. "Did you find the papers?"

"Yes," Nancy managed to answer. Her heart was pounding. Even though Jon couldn't see her, she felt as though she'd been caught. "I'll be right back. I was just heading out the door."

She waited for him to say that the errand seemed to be taking a long time. Instead, he said, "Good. It's starting to get busy and the other waitresses are complaining."

"I'll hurry," Nancy promised. She hung up, grabbed the papers, and left.

When Nancy reached Moves, things were already jumping. The music was wild and loud, and the dance floor was filling up.

Jon's backup deejay was in the sound booth, so Nancy went back to Jon's office, the envelope under her arm. She rapped lightly at the door.

"Come in," she heard a weary, discouraged voice say.

Nancy stepped inside to find Jon sitting behind his desk. There was no sign of Laurie. "Here are the papers you wanted," Nancy said, laying the manila envelope and keys down in front of her boss.

Jon didn't seem to be in any particular hurry to open the envelope. He just looked at it dully.

"Thanks," he said with a long sigh.

"I'd better get to work," Nancy replied.

Jon only nodded, staring off into space. He looked worried, but that was no surprise to Nancy, considering what she'd learned from that partially finished letter he'd written to an uncle. He owed money to the wrong people, and he didn't know how he was going to pay.

Nancy waited tables until the club closed. Then, as she was leaving, she decided to ask George and Bess to meet her back at her house, to get their advice about the case. Nancy knew Ned had to work the next day and didn't bother him. For once, Nancy seemed to have too many clues and not enough theories.

"Well, I've had a productive evening," she told her two friends after they were settled in with a late-night snack of soft drinks and pizza. She told them about the errand she had had to run for Jon.

George looked surprised. "Wow! So you had a chance to check out his place."

"Yeah. But I'm not sure why he really sent me," Nancy mused. She shook her head. "It was all very weird."

Bess was practically falling out of her chair with impatience. "So what did you find?" she demanded.

Nancy helped herself to another bite of pizza and chewed and swallowed before answering. "Well, I found some letters—love letters from somebody named Sheila. She wrote faithfully for months, but, according to the dates, stopped writing for about two years. Then just recently, she started again, as if nothing had happened."

"Was there anything important about the letters?" George wanted to know.

Nancy shrugged. "Not unless I missed something. Whoever Sheila is, though, she and Jon must have been serious about each other. She talked about how much she loved him and how she couldn't wait to be his wife."

"Maybe he's married!" Bess cried suddenly. "Oh, poor Laurie—she's so crazy about this guy and he turns out to be a married man!"

George rolled her eyes. "Aren't you jumping to conclusions here?" she asked. "There's no proof

Jon and Sheila ever got married. She's still writing to him, which should indicate just the opposite."

Bess subsided. "Well, it's possible," she insisted stubbornly.

Nancy continued going over the facts of the case. "Jon's got a police record. He owes somebody money, and he needs more time to come up with it—"

George interrupted. "Wait a minute. What's this about him owing someone money?"

Nancy quickly explained about Jon's unfinished letter to his uncle Mike.

Bess ticked the facts off on her fingers. "He's a crook, the mob is out to get him, and somebody named Sheila wrote him a stack of mushy letters."

"Letters he valued enough to keep," George mused, frowning.

"We aren't getting anywhere with this," Bess said, and much as Nancy hated to admit it, she knew her friend was right. She'd gathered together several pieces to the puzzle, but none of them fit.

"I know this much," Nancy said. "I've got to talk to Laurie the first chance I get."

"Are you going to warn her to stay away from Jon?" Bess asked.

Nancy sighed. "I think I'd better tell her what I know, at least. And I want to ask her a few questions to find out what she knows. She's been hiding something from me all along."

George nodded and closed the lid on the empty pizza box. "We could help you out, if you want," she offered. George was always volunteering Bess for things, but her pretty blond cousin didn't seem to mind.

Nancy shook her head. "Thanks, but there's no sense in getting her mad at all three of us. I'll take care of it."

Laurie didn't return any of Nancy's calls the next day. Finally, Nancy drove over to the Weavers'. She was determined to get through to Laurie somehow.

When Nancy arrived, she found Laurie sitting on the porch, all dressed up. She was wearing a sleeveless, V-necked dress made from the most delicate pink silk Nancy had ever seen.

"Hi," Nancy said.

For a moment she didn't think Laurie was going to speak to her but, finally, she said, "Hello, Nancy. What are you doing here?"

"You and I have to talk," Nancy told her.

Laurie looked past Nancy to the big circular driveway, then glanced down at her expensive watch. "Sorry," she said coolly. "No time. I have a date."

Nancy sighed. "We've known each other a long time, Laurie."

"Then you should know if I asked you to stop doing something, you should trust my judgment," Laurie said accusingly. "Instead, you go sneaking around behind my boyfriend's back. Don't think I don't know why you wormed your way into that job at Moves, Nancy!"

Nancy was quiet for a moment. Then she said, "You didn't tell Jon that I'm a detective, did you?"

Laurie refused to look at Nancy, but she shook her head. "No. I didn't tell."

"Why not?" Nancy asked softly.

"Because I knew you wouldn't find out anything bad about Jon."

"I did, though, Laurie," Nancy said. "Did you know he has a police record?"

Color pulsed in Laurie's cheeks. "Shhh!" she said angrily. "If my parents hear about that, they'll have a fit!"

I was right, Nancy thought, without satisfaction. She does know a few things about Jon's past. "Doesn't it bother you that Jon is a convicted felon?" she persisted, keeping her voice down.

"He's changed," Laurie insisted. "Besides, he's paid for his crime. He was in jail for two years."

That accounted for the time between Sheila's letters, Nancy reflected. Either he hadn't been able to keep them, or she'd stopped writing while he was in prison.

"I think Jon might be in deep trouble," Nancy went on gently. "I know he needs money. And your family has it. Laurie, have you ever thought that he could be using you? He could be planning—"

"I don't want to hear this!" Laurie cried, clasping her hands over her ears and walking around the side of the house.

Nancy followed her, but there was no way she could force Laurie to listen.

"He's coming here tonight," Laurie said after taking a moment to calm down. "He's going to have dinner with us and get to know my parents better, and I won't let anybody spoil this evening —including you, Nancy."

Nancy sighed. There was no point in trying to convince Laurie that Jon Villiers might be bad news. She said goodbye to her friend and was just turning to walk away when the sprinkler system came on.

Behind her, Nancy heard Laurie scream. She turned to see Laurie standing absolutely still, helpless and drenched. Her silk outfit appeared to be ruined by the water. Nancy grabbed her arm, and they both dashed out of range of the sprinklers.

"What—" Laurie was practically speechless.

"It was probably just a neighbor kid," Nancy said to Laurie, "I'll check it out." With that, she hurried around the back of the house.

Although Nancy circled the mansion, she saw no one. There were just too many places to hide.

When she got back to the front, Laurie was still standing on the porch, shivering.

"The whole evening is ruined," she complained to Nancy. She looked as though she was on the verge of tears. "My hair, my dress . . ."

"Come on," Nancy said gently. "We'll go inside and you can change."

Laurie hastily put on another outfit. While Nancy was drying off, the telephone beside Laurie's bed rang, and she pounced on it.

Nancy knew what was happening before a word was spoken on that end of the line. Laurie's face crumpled with disappointment.

"Oh, Jon, I was counting on your being here," she said finally. "This has been the worst evening. . . . I understand. Good night."

Nancy left with only a quiet goodbye. Anything she said would have only made things worse for Laurie.

When Nancy arrived at Moves, the lot was crowded and she had to park a long way from the door. Angry voices alerted her to an argument going on nearby, though she couldn't quite make out the words.

Seeing Jon and Pam a few yards away, she crouched low and stayed on the opposite side of a row of cars so they wouldn't see her.

Unfortunately, she could only make out a few words of their conversation. She heard *Laurie* and *love*. Then, suddenly Pam's voice rose to an angry shout.

"Don't think you're going to get away with this!" she said.

Jon looked alarmed. "Please—"

Pam burst into tears. "I can make sure your precious Laurie never wants to lay eyes on you again," she sobbed. "And I will, Jon—I'll make sure she knows it all! I'll tell her *everything!*"

Chapter
Eight

Pᴀᴍ's ᴡᴏʀᴅs ᴇᴄʜᴏᴇᴅ in Nancy's mind as she watched Jon turn away from the waitress and stride back into the club. I'll make sure she knows it all. . . . I'll tell her everything. . . .

But what was "everything?"

That's the million-dollar question, Nancy thought. That could be the key to this whole mystery.

Nancy sneaked back to her car, opened the door, and slammed it to let Pam know she wasn't alone in the parking lot. Nancy also wanted the waitress to think she'd just arrived and couldn't have overheard the conversation.

"Hi, Pam," she said cheerfully, strolling up to her.

Pam didn't pay any attention to her for several moments—she was still staring after Jon. Finally when she turned her head toward Nancy, there was a dazed look in her eyes. "Hi," she answered at last.

Nancy wanted to put an arm around the girl and reassure her, she looked so downhearted, but she kept her distance. "Are you okay?" Nancy asked, pretending that she'd just noticed Pam's tear-streaked face and puffy eyes.

"Yeah," Pam said a little defensively. "I'm okay."

Nancy thought of another scene she'd witnessed, when Jon and Pam had been dancing together and Pam had gotten angry and called Jon a criminal. "Listen, if you feel like talking . . ."

Pam looked at Nancy for a long moment. A thought flickered across her eyes, then was gone. She started toward the club.

Nancy fell into step beside her. She wanted to find out what Pam knew about Jon—obviously, it was a lot—but she felt sorry for the girl, too. She was in a lot of pain.

"I just had a big fight with Jon," Pam said when they'd reached the side entrance to the club. She paused, just outside the door, and so did Nancy.

73

Nancy pretended surprise. "Oh?"

Pam angrily folded her arms across her chest. "He's such a jerk. He's been coming on to me behind Laurie's back for so long—" She stopped, shook her head, then went on.

"But of course he doesn't want to break up with Laurie—or with her money. Well, I'm not interested in a guy like him. I warned him tonight—I'm going to tell her everything if he doesn't leave me alone!"

Nancy was taken aback. For some reason she'd gotten the impression that it was the other way around—that Pam was the one after Jon. They obviously knew each other better than they'd let on. Nancy had assumed that Pam was an old girlfriend, and that Jon had dumped her.

But maybe she was wrong. After all, Jon had been alone with Pam, dancing with her, holding her tenderly in his arms, that first time Nancy had seen them together.

Nancy thought of the letters hidden away in Jon's apartment, from someone named Sheila Day. The last one, full of heartbreak and desperate pleas, was dated only two months earlier. Evidently Jon worked fast. He broke Sheila's heart, and now he was on his way to breaking Laurie's, too, with Pam.

Another waitress appeared at the door, interrupting Nancy's thoughts. "Will you two please hurry up?" she fretted. "We need help in here!"

Before Pam could lash out, as the expression on her face indicated she would, Nancy said, "We'll be right in."

After the other waitress left, Nancy put her hand lightly on Pam's arm. "I'll cover for you while you take a few minutes to pull yourself together," she said.

Pam looked at her in surprise. "Thanks" was all she said. Moments later Nancy was hard at work, and after about ten minutes, Pam joined her.

"Hi." Ned took a table in Nancy's section of the club a couple of hours later. He grinned as Nancy walked over to him with her pad and pencil.

"What'll it be, fella?" Nancy asked, putting a twang in her voice and pretending to chew gum.

Ned laughed and ordered a soda and a hamburger with everything. When Nancy came back with his food, it was time for her break, so she joined him at the table.

"Are you supposed to be this friendly with the customers?" Ned teased.

Nancy spotted George and Bess and waved them over to Ned's table. "Only good-looking captains of the Emerson College football team get this kind of treatment," she answered before Bess and George pulled up chairs opposite Ned and Nancy.

"So, what's happening?" George wanted to know.

Nancy sighed. "All I'm getting out of this investigation is minimum wage and sore feet," she complained.

A young man came to the table and asked Bess to dance. She was gone in a flash. George watched her cousin disappear into the crush on the dance floor with laughter in her dark eyes. "It's a good thing we can count on Bess to stand by us and keep her mind on the case no matter what," she joked.

Nancy helped herself to one of Ned's french fries. "But when the chips are down," she pointed out, "Bess Marvin always comes through."

"True," George admitted.

"Do you have time for a dance, Nancy?" Ned asked, pushing away the plastic basket that had contained his hamburger and fries.

Nancy consulted her watch. "If it's short," she answered.

Ned stood up and took her elbow lightly in his hand, squiring her toward the dance floor. "It's not against the rules, then?"

Nancy smiled. "If it is, I'll hear about it," she answered. The music was slow and romantic, and she moved easily into Ned's arms. She gave a happy sigh.

"How about an update on the case?" he asked, while they danced.

Nancy told him about being sent to Jon's apartment for papers and finding the love letters.

"Jon must have been in pretty deep with this Sheila woman," Ned observed.

Nancy nodded her agreement. "The letters went back a long time, though there was a two-year gap. Probably that was when Jon was in prison."

Ned stiffened slightly. "I don't like the idea of your working for somebody with a record," he said.

"People change," Nancy pointed out.

"Not all that much," Ned replied.

Just then the music ended and so did Nancy's break. When she went back to work, Ned stayed. Nancy could tell he was worried about her safety and wanted to keep an eye on her.

When the time came for Nancy's next break, Adam Boyd was waiting for her.

"I'd like to talk to you," he said grimly.

As far as Nancy was concerned, Adam was still a suspect in what was going on. But she wouldn't be doing her job if she didn't listen to what Adam had to say. "Sure," she answered.

They went into the front entryway, where it was relatively private.

"How do you like working for such a lowlife?" he asked.

Nancy drew back from him, angry. "I didn't come out here to listen to this, Adam," she said, turning away.

Adam reached out and took a rather desperate hold of Nancy's arm. A hard stare from her made him let go.

He sighed heavily and ran one hand through his hair. "I'm sorry. It's just that I can't seem to get anybody to listen."

Nancy felt a twinge of sympathy for Adam. He cared deeply for Laurie, and the break-up had been hard for him. "Sometimes it's just better to admit it's over," she said quietly. "Just forget it and go on from here. After all, there's lots of girls who'd like to date you."

Adam took hold of her arm again, though this time his touch was light. "You're Laurie's friend, Nancy. Please talk to her, try to reason with her—"

"I can't change her feelings, Adam," Nancy said. "Nobody can do that."

"You don't trust him, either," Adam said. "That's why you're working here. You're trying to find out what he's up to."

Nancy hoped Jon wouldn't come to the same conclusion. But then he wasn't from River Heights and wouldn't know about her detective work as Adam did. She tried to soothe Adam.

"I've tried to talk to Laurie," she said, "and she wouldn't listen. Trust me, I won't give up until I find out what's going on here and who's behind it."

That last part was more than a statement, it was a warning, and it was clear that Adam understood that. He let go of Nancy's arm and some of the color drained from his face. Just then, the door opened and Laurie came in, looking especially pretty in a new sundress. She smiled at Nancy as though nothing had happened between them, but she didn't so much as look at Adam.

"Is Jon in the booth?" she asked.

Nancy glanced at Adam, who was back to looking angry and sullen, before answering. "Yes."

"I can't wait to see him," Laurie beamed. Then, still ignoring Adam, she hurried eagerly into the main part of the club.

When Nancy looked back at Adam, he was staring after Laurie with such fury in his eyes that she was alarmed. "Let's go, Adam," she said in a quiet, reasonable voice.

Adam's jaw was set in a hard line as he glared at her. "Leave me alone," he snarled, "or you're going to be very sorry!" With that, he turned and pushed back into the club.

Nancy's second and last break was over, so she had to go back to work. She cleared several tables and started for the kitchen, thinking of Adam's warning. Had he been threatening her?

Since her hands were full, Nancy shouldered her way through the opening. Once inside she was met with a roaring sound, then a blinding light from the deep fat fryers, which were just to her right. Nancy dropped her tray, sending it clattering to the floor.

The kitchen's fryer was shooting off needle-sharp sprays of burning-hot grease!

Chapter

Nine

Nancy gasped, then started to cough as a billow of greasy black smoke rolled toward her. Eyes watering, she tried to peer around the kitchen. Was anyone else in there?

"Help!" came one of the cook's voices. "I'm trapped back here!"

Nancy could see her, the head cook, the one she had talked to, huddled by the big range. Pulling off her apron, Nancy used it to shield her face as she ran past the steaming fryer. She grabbed the cook's arm.

"Cover your face," she yelled. "Let's go—the whole thing may catch fire any second."

Still clutching the cook's arm, Nancy ducked past the fryer again. She bit off a cry of pain as the grease spattered her bare arm.

She dragged the cook from the kitchen. By this time, smoke detectors were madly screaming alarms throughout the club.

Ned pushed through the small crowd to stand beside Nancy. His face was grim.

"Are you hurt?" he gasped.

Before Nancy could answer, Pam Hastings rushed past them with a fire extinguisher. She stopped cold when she saw Nancy's grease-covered apron.

Jon appeared then, too, his face pale. "What's happening?" he cried, taking the extinguisher from Pam and tearing into the kitchen as fire sirens screamed outside.

After the fire was out, Jon joined the others in the hall.

"This does it," the cook sputtered. "Mr. Villiers, I quit." She threw down her apron.

"Wait a second, Carol," Jon pleaded. "Can't we please talk about this? Here, we can step into my office——" Still talking, he led the cook away, throwing an apologetic look over his shoulder.

In the crowd that had gathered behind them, Nancy spotted Laurie and Bess and George. But there was no sign of Adam.

"Maybe you'd better go home for the rest of

the night," Pam said, looking Nancy over with a frown.

Nancy shook her head. She wasn't hurt; she would stay until the end of the shift because she meant to look into this "accident."

"If there's another apron I could use—"

Pam's expression was disapproving, but she nodded and disappeared into a stock room. In a few moments, she returned with another apron and a new Moves T-shirt.

"You're sure you want to stick around?" Ned pressed, looking worried.

Nancy nodded. "I'm sure," she said, heading for the ladies' room to change. George and Bess followed her to supervise.

"It looks like somebody deliberately tried to cook you," George pointed out.

"But how would anyone know I was going into the kitchen just then?" Nancy countered logically. "And what happened to the person? How did he or she get out?"

Then Nancy thought of Adam again. Had he been angry enough to do something so risky and dangerous?

"Maybe it was an accident," she said, but somehow she doubted it. She washed her hands and face and then, with George and Bess following right behind her, she set out for the kitchen. Jon was there, talking to Pam and the head cook, whom he seemed to have persuaded to stay.

"Are you all right?" he demanded, when he saw Nancy.

"I don't have any idea how this could have happened," fussed the cook. "The fryer is supposed to have a regulator to keep it from overheating. I've never seen anything like that."

"Me, either," agreed Pam, who was a little pale.

"How did you get here with the extinguisher so quickly?" Nancy asked her.

"I was just coming in to pick up an order," Pam said. "I was right behind you and saw the whole thing. So I ran for an extinguisher in the club."

Nancy glanced at the clock. She wanted to find out who had set this fire. "I guess I'd better get back to work now," she said, thinking about other possible leads.

Jon stared at her. "Work? After what you've been through? Nancy, I want you to go home for the night."

"It's only twenty minutes until quitting time," Nancy argued politely. "And I'm not hurt. I'd like to stay."

Jon shrugged looking baffled. "Have it your own way," he said and walked out.

Nancy hurried back to the main part of the club with George and Bess right behind her.

"We'll each take a third of the room," Nancy

whispered. "I want to know if Adam Boyd is still around."

As Nancy worked her way through the crowd, several people stopped her to ask if she was all right. She spotted Ned, sitting alone at a table, and she saw concern in his eyes.

"I'm fine," she mouthed, but he only shook his head.

When Bess, George, and Nancy met again, they exchanged the same story. There was no sign of Adam Boyd. He was gone.

The next morning Bess and George dragged Nancy off to the mall for what Bess called a "relaxation session." This consisted mostly of window-shopping and listening to Bess rave about the cute guys they saw. Ordinarily, Nancy would have enjoyed herself, but that day she couldn't keep her mind off the case.

"I can't believe you're actually going back to that place after what happened," Bess protested. "You could have been scarred for life—or even killed!"

"But I wasn't," Nancy pointed out reasonably.

"Which only means that you might not be so lucky next time," Bess replied.

After checking out the music store and renting a video, the girls went into a restaurant for an early lunch.

"Maybe the fire really was an accident," George speculated, as she munched on her bacon, lettuce, and tomato sandwich.

Bess shook her head. "It wasn't any more of an accident than the noose on Laurie's porch or the message on the answering machine or the slashed tires. Somebody almost drowned Nancy, and now he's tried to barbecue her!"

Nancy couldn't help chuckling at Bess's dramatic way of looking at things. "I have a feeling you're right, Bess. But I am going to solve this mystery, no matter what."

Nancy arrived at work on the stroke of seven that night. With Bess and George she wanted to let Jon know that she was all right—he'd seemed so worried about her the night before—so she headed straight for his office.

Just as she was turning the corner into the hall, however, she caught the scent of cigar smoke and stopped. A tough-looking, middle-aged man was just stepping into Jon's office. He pulled the door closed behind him.

Something about the man's expression told Nancy that his business with Jon might be worth listening to. She crept up to the door, crouched down in front of it so that her shadow wouldn't show through the frosted glass, and peered through the keyhole.

The man with the cigar looked about fifty years

old. His suit was shabby and his shoes were in desperate need of a polish. He was surrounded by a cloud of smoke.

"I'm telling you, boy, you've either got to pay up or get the job done," he was saying to Jon. "I can't hold these guys off forever, you know."

The man turned in Nancy's direction, and thinking he might open the door and discover her there, Nancy darted away. She was smoothing her apron when Adam Boyd appeared in the main hallway beside her. Nancy didn't want Jon and his visitor to find her there, but she couldn't just ignore Adam.

"I've been looking for you," he said.

Nancy stood still, searching his face. Was he capable of hurting someone? She said nothing, waiting for him to go on.

"I heard about the accident last night," Adam went on. There was nothing in his expression except sympathy and relief. "I'm glad you weren't hurt, Nancy." He sounded so sincere that Nancy let down her guard a little. Still, she didn't want Jon and the man with the cigar to find them in the hallway, so she took Adam's arm and ushered him down the hall closer to the main club.

"I want to apologize. I've acted like a real jerk," Adam admitted to Nancy. "It's just that Laurie meant so much to me."

Nancy looked closely at Adam. Had she been wrong about him?

"It's not easy to lose someone you care about," Nancy said sympathetically. She hesitated.

"Adam, can I ask you one question?" He nodded, and Nancy went on. "A few nights ago I saw you give Pam some money. Why did you do that?" she asked, deciding to be direct.

Adam looked blank. "Huh? When? Oh, the only time I remember is that night when I chewed your ear off about Laurie and Villiers? Let's see? I just asked Pam to make some change. All I had was a twenty, and I wanted to leave her a tip. She didn't have the right change on her, so she brought it to me later."

Nancy smiled. One small mystery solved. But a glance at her watch told her it was time to start working.

She said a quick goodbye to Adam and then almost hit Ned when she pushed open the door. Adam breezed quickly by both of them. "Were you talking to Adam?" he wanted to know.

Nancy grinned up at him. "Jealous, Nickerson?"

Ned scowled. He obviously wasn't in the mood to be teased. "You told me you suspect Adam of being behind some of the stuff that's been happening lately. Don't you think it would be a good idea to stay away from him?"

"I now think Adam is innocent. But how can I

find out anything if I avoid everybody?" Nancy reasoned.

Ned sighed. "I guess you can't."

"I'll be careful," Nancy promised.

"Sometimes that isn't enough," Ned replied, obviously thinking of the incident the night before.

Nancy knew it was time to change the subject. "Oh, look," she said, smiling. "There's George and Bess."

Ned grumbled something, but when the girls came over to them, he warmed up. In fact, since Nancy had to work, he asked Bess to dance.

Nancy took the opportunity to work her way back toward Jon's office, hoping to hear what Jon and the strange man were saying. She was distracted, however, when a disturbance broke out in the dancing area.

Nancy ran back and watched as people were pushing and shoving to escape the room's three exits. Smoke was billowing up from the floor. Then a voice screamed a single word over the din.

"Fire!"

Chapter

Ten

F**IRE! N**ANCY'S **HEART STOPPED.** The club was so crowded, it would be almost impossible to keep order until everyone was safely out.

A glance around the club confirmed her worst suspicions. She scanned the crowd and saw George, Bess, and Ned all making their way to her from different directions. The exits were jammed and people were being pushed down and stepped on in the rush to escape.

"At this rate," Bess said, shouting to be heard, "nobody's going to get out of here alive!"

"We need to cover the doors," Nancy shouted back. "And make sure people keep moving without pushing and shoving." The smoke was getting so thick her eyes were stinging.

George and Bess went off to cover the side door. Ned pulled Nancy into his arms and hugged her hard.

"Be careful" was all he said. Then he pushed his way through the crush to the front door.

Nancy made her way toward the back. The hallway and kitchen were packed. She started urging the frightened kids through the delivery door in a brisk and orderly manner, and her natural authority made them listen and clear a path for her.

"Take it easy," she repeated over and over. "It'll be okay."

After what seemed an eternity everyone was out. Nancy decided to make one last check of the hallway. The smoke was dense there, but she was glad she'd taken the time to investigate because she spotted Pam Hastings at the top of the basement steps, gripping the doorknob and coughing. The girl couldn't move.

"Pam!" Nancy cried, coughing hard herself as she dashed to the other waitress. "Come on— you've got to get out of here!"

Pam just shook her head weakly. Alarmed, Nancy put one arm around her waist and practically carried her down the hall. Outside she could hear fire engines arriving, their sirens wailing.

Nancy's eyes and throat were burning badly by

the time she reached the kitchen. She was just about to burst out into the fresh air when she heard a muffled and hoarse voice call for help. The shout came from deep inside the club.

Nancy hesitated. Her lungs were screaming for air, but she couldn't make herself go. Not when she knew someone was still inside.

"Go on, Pam," she croaked, shoving Pam through the doorway.

Nancy gulped in a couple of lungfuls of fresh air before hurrying back into the club. She slithered along so that most of the smoke rolled over her. It was like a black, acrid cloud now, and she could barely see.

"Help me!" the voice cried again. "Somebody —please—"

"Where are you?" Nancy called, pushing through the swinging doors that led into the dancing area.

"Over—over here—"

Nancy followed the weak voice between small pockets of flames. "I can't see you! The smoke is too thick."

"Here—here, by the sound booth—"

Nancy found Adam Boyd on the floor, struggling to stand. Obviously he'd been knocked down by someone rushing to escape. He was still dazed.

While Nancy was using all her strength to help Adam up, he collapsed and fell unconscious. She dragged him and groped her way to the front door, where firefighters were storming through with hoses and equipment.

Seeing that Nancy was in trouble, one firefighter rushed over and hoisted the unconscious Adam over one shoulder. "Follow me, miss. Get out of here fast," he shouted over the roar of water and fire.

"Laurie." Adam woke up and choked out the single word.

"Where?" Nancy asked.

"Laurie's in there somewhere—I saw her—"

Nancy went outside and stood gasping for air while she scanned the crowd gathered to watch the firemen battle the blaze. There was no sign of Laurie anywhere.

Before anyone could stop her, Nancy raced back into the club, zigzagging between areas of now-raging flames. She had to find Laurie!

"Laurie!" Nancy shouted, making a quick round of the dance floor and the area behind the sound booth. The name seemed to tear at her throat. "Laurie!"

No answer.

With her apron over her face to filter out some of the smoke, Nancy raced toward the back of the club and Jon's office.

"Laurie!" she cried, bursting through the doorway to the office, which the fire had spared so far.

It was there that she thought she heard a whimpering sound, barely audible.

"Laurie, where are you?" Nancy called, desperation in her voice.

She heard the sound again and, after a quick check of the room, realized that it was coming up through the heating vent in the floor. She dropped to her knees and called through the grating. "Laurie, it's Nancy. Can you hear me?"

The reply was faint. "Nancy——"

Laurie was trapped in the basement! Nancy ran out into the hallway and raced toward the cellar stairs. She tore down seven steps but was stopped by a locked door at the bottom.

Nancy doubled up both fists and pounded on the heavy wooden obstacle. "Laurie!" she called, choking out the name. "Laurie, open the door!"

"I can't," Laurie replied from the other side. Her voice sounded weak.

Remembering that Jon always left an extra set of keys on his desk, Nancy fled back up the stairs to the office. The hallway was becoming impassable now; the fire had spread there, too.

Nancy ran her hands over the surface of Jon's desk and then plundered the drawers in search of his key ring. In the last drawer she found it. She was back at the cellar door within seconds, frantically trying one key after another.

But key after key failed to open the lock. Nancy fought against the panic that threatened her. If she lost her head now, she and Laurie would both die.

At last Nancy found the key that fitted the lock on the cellar door. She felt relief sweep through her when the knob turned in her hand.

The basement was dark, but the smoke wasn't bad. Nancy stepped inside.

"Laurie!" she cried, coughing.

A groan came from somewhere in the shadows.

Nancy flipped the light switch beside the door, but nothing happened. Obviously, the fire had already destroyed the building's electrical system. Nancy began to grope, calling her friend's name over and over again as she screamed in the pitch darkness.

She stumbled over Laurie, lying prone on the floor. Before she could lift her, Nancy heard the cellar door swing shut with a solid thud.

"Oh, no," Nancy whispered as a terrible possibility struck her. She made her way back to the door and tried the knob. It wouldn't turn.

Behind her, Laurie was stirring in the darkness. "Nancy? Oh, my head—"

"Help!" Nancy yelled, hoping that one of the firemen would hear. She battered at the door with both fists and shouted again. "Help!"

"My head—hurts—I think somebody hit me," Laurie was saying in a dazed voice.

Nancy rested her forehead against the heavy door for the brief moment, breathing hard, struggling to calm herself. When she laid both palms against the wood, she realized that the door was still cool. The fire hadn't gotten any closer yet. The smoke wasn't as bad as it was in the hallway, either.

She turned, her eyes slowly adjusting to the darkness, to see Laurie sitting up, one hand pressed to her head.

"Wh-what's going on?" Nancy's friend asked.

"We're in big trouble," she answered quietly. "The club's on fire and we're locked in down here."

"Help!" Laurie screamed.

"I tried that," Nancy said. "No one's going to hear us. We've got to find another way out."

Laurie was too scared to be of any help. Spider webs draped themselves over Nancy's arms and hair as she searched, exploring the walls for a window. If there were any, they were either painted or boarded over.

"What's going to happen to us?" Laurie moaned.

Nancy didn't want to think about the answer to that question. She began going over the floor for something she could use to pry open the door.

"Nancy, what's going to happen to us?" Laurie repeated, sounding even more scared than before. Nancy didn't blame her for being frightened, but she knew her friend had to keep her head.

"We're going to get out of here," Nancy said, still searching. She went to lay her hands against the door again, checking it for heat. It felt disturbingly warm now. "Somehow, we're going to find a way out."

The calm resolution in Nancy's voice must have comforted Laurie, because she got up and began running her hands over the walls, looking for a way to escape.

Smoke was coming in beneath the door now. Nancy found an old potato sack and tried to block up the crack. The fire was close now. It was getting hard to breathe.

Nancy knew their time had almost run out.

Chapter

Eleven

NANCY COULDN'T GIVE UP. With tears streaming down her cheeks from the smoke, she groped along the cellar walls. Suddenly she bumped into a large filing cabinet. Running her fingers behind it, she felt something sticking out from the wall. Could it be—?

"I think there's a window behind this cabinet!" Nancy cried out excitedly. "Come on, Laurie, let's try to move this out of the way—"

The smoke was thick in the room now, and the heat of the fire was heavy. Nancy felt as though she was smothering.

But the two girls pushed and shoved until the

cabinet had been moved aside. Behind it was a grimy, narrow little window.

Nancy wiped the window with her sleeve and saw booted feet outside. Firefighters! She grabbed the casement in both hands and rattled it. "Help!" she cried with Laurie joining in.

The firefighters heard them. One knelt and shouted, "Stand back from the window and cover your heads!"

Nancy put an arm around Laurie's waist and the two of them stepped back with their backs to the window, their arms covering their faces. The splintering of glass was a welcome sound.

By now, Laurie was only half-conscious. One firefighter lifted her out through the opening where the window had been and carried her a safe distance from the endangered building. Another helped Nancy to scramble out. She coughed as the clean air reached her lungs.

"Is anybody still inside?" she asked one of the firefighters.

"Except for Mr. Villiers, you and your friend were the last. Maybe you should sit down for a minute, miss."

Nancy shook her head, scanning the crowd for Ned, Bess, and George. She knew her friends would be worried and wanted to reassure them as soon as possible. Starting toward her car, she passed Pam Hastings.

Pam's sooty face was streaked with tears as she

stared bleakly at the building. Quiet sobs shook her shoulders.

Nancy had just spotted her friends when there was an outburst of cheering behind her. She turned to see Jon being led out of the building by two firefighters. His clothes were torn and sooty, but even from a distance Nancy could tell he was fine.

She was glad he was safe, but it did seem odd that, although he'd been inside the burning building the longest of anyone, he was relatively clean and uninjured. What had he been doing in there?

And what about Laurie? How had she gotten locked in the cellar? And how had she been dazed?

Nancy didn't like the conclusions she was coming to, but she couldn't ignore them. Laurie had nearly died and not by accident. Someone had locked her in the cellar, while the building was going up in flames. That same someone may have set the fire in the first place.

"Nancy!" Ned interrupted her thoughts. He took her shoulders in his hands and looked down at her face. "Are you all right?" Nancy nodded.

Bess and George ran up then, too. "What happened?" George wanted to know.

"We were about to go back in there for you!" Bess cried.

Nancy let out a long sigh and ran one hand

through her hair. Looking at her fingers, she realized that she was probably covered with black soot from head to toe. She explained how she had found Adam and then Laurie.

"You found her in the cellar?" Ned said, his hands still gripping Nancy's shoulders firmly.

"I know it's strange, but it seems as if someone could have hit her over the head and left her there. . . ."

There was a stunned silence while Bess, George, and Ned absorbed what Nancy had said.

"That's terrible," whispered Bess.

"That same person could have set the fire," George speculated.

"Right," Nancy agreed. She glanced back at the building. Laurie was sitting up on the grass now, a paramedic kneeling beside her, waiting to see if she needed more oxygen.

Nancy and the others made their way through the crowd to Laurie's side, but Jon had reached her first. He was holding her as though he would never let her go, when Nancy joined them.

Laurie looked up at Nancy with an expression of both sadness and fear in her eyes. "If it hadn't been for you—" she started, but Nancy silenced her with a shake of her head.

"You would have done the same for me," she said.

"I'm not sure I would have been brave enough," Laurie replied. She was standing upright now and leaning against Jon for support. "Thank you, Nancy. Thank you for saving my life."

"It's okay, Laurie," Nancy said quietly. "Just tell me what happened. Did you hear anyone—see anyone?"

Laurie was shaking her head. "No. The last thing I remember is standing in the hallway outside Jon's office. There was this sudden pain at the back of my head, then everything went black. Next thing I knew, you were calling to me from somewhere."

Nancy was disappointed, but not surprised. She'd had a feeling that Laurie had been attacked and couldn't have seen her attacker. She turned her gaze to Jon. "You were in the building a long time," she observed.

Jon looked confused, tired, and relieved. "I was looking for Laurie. I guess I just checked all the wrong places. Thanks for finding her, Nancy."

Nancy nodded and turned away, exhausted. She would sort through everything later—all she wanted at that moment was a hot bath, a few of Hannah's cookies, and a good night's sleep. Ned's arm was strong around her waist.

"Once again," remarked a shrill feminine voice, "our own Nancy Drew is at center stage. You're a regular Wonder Woman."

Nancy couldn't believe her bad luck. Standing

before her was Brenda Carlton. She and Ned started to move around the young reporter, but Brenda blocked their way.

"Exactly what happened here tonight?" she demanded.

Nancy gave her a wry smile. "I would think that would be obvious, Brenda," she said sweetly. Nancy lowered her voice to a confidential whisper, and leaned toward Brenda as though to share a big secret. "There was a fire."

Brenda's face puckered with annoyance. "I know that!" she sputtered.

"Nothing gets by you, does it, Brenda?" George asked.

By this time Brenda had recovered her composure. "Not much," she said, smoothing the lapels of her jacket. Then she shoved past Nancy to Jon.

Flashes blinded everyone within a dozen feet as Brenda's photographer snapped pictures of Laurie and Jon. The light of the blaze made it seem like midday. "What started this fire, Mr. Villiers?" Brenda asked, rapid-fire. "Or, should I say, *who* started this fire?"

The color drained from Jon's face. "I don't know," he said. "It must have been an accident."

"An accident?" Brenda repeated, raising one eyebrow.

Laurie huddled close to Jon, looking baffled and afraid. Nancy knew her friend didn't believe the fire had been an accident. Neither had the blow to Laurie's head. "Can't we all go home and forget about this?" she asked Brenda. "It's been an awful night, after all—"

"I'll be happy to answer your questions some other time," Jon said, putting an arm around Laurie and starting to walk away.

Brenda stopped them easily. "I've been doing some research on you, Mr. Villiers," she said, but she tossed a malicious smile in Nancy's direction even as she spoke. "It seems you had a whole other life in Chicago."

Jon stopped, his back rigid. Nancy watched as he turned slowly to face Brenda.

"Please," he said hoarsely. "Don't. Not now, not tonight."

But Brenda was on a roll and she wasn't about to back down. "It seems that Mr. Villiers is a star," she announced to the crowd gathered around. "I can call you Jon, can't I—Jon?"

Some of the tension seemed to leave Jon. He sighed and shrugged wearily. Laurie was looking up at him.

Nancy took Brenda by the arm and pulled her aside, where they could talk privately. "What's going on here, Brenda?" she demanded. "Why did you say Jon is a star?"

Brenda examined her perfectly manicured fingernails. She didn't like giving Nancy information, but apparently her need to feel important got the best of her. "I got curious about Jon

Villiers and checked back issues of the Chicago newspapers. Jon was a celebrity of sorts. He and his partner, Sheila Day, were big on the dance circuit in the Windy City a few years ago. They got a lot of publicity and won a few prizes—things like that. He and the girl were a sensation."

"Sheila Day," Nancy muttered to herself, remembering the love letters she'd found in Jon's apartment. "Thanks, Brenda."

Brenda scowled at her and walked back to the others. Nancy returned to Ned's side.

Brenda had taken up her questioning again. "Weren't you a professional dancer, Mr. Villiers?"

Jon looked down at Laurie for a moment before answering, in a bleak tone. "Yes. But I don't see what that has to do with anything—"

Laurie was still gazing up at Jon.

"You had a partner, a Sheila Day, right?"

"Yes."

"There was a rumor you were engaged to be married. Whatever happened between you two?"

Jon sighed. "I haven't seen Sheila—or heard from her—in over two years. Just leave me alone, will you?" With that, Jon put his arm around Laurie again and hurried off.

Nancy watched them walk away. She knew Jon was lying about not being in touch with Sheila. The last of her letters had been dated only a couple of months earlier. What was he covering up?

"Let's go," Ned said softly, interrupting her thoughts. "It's late."

Nancy nodded and said, "Goodbye, Brenda. And thanks for the help."

Brenda was steaming, but Nancy only smiled at her and then walked beside Ned to her car, Bess and George trailing behind them.

"Maybe I'd better drive," George suggested.

Suddenly Nancy was very tired. "That sounds good to me," she said.

Ned gave her a light kiss on the forehead. "Your adventures are going to be the death of me, Drew," he said with a sigh.

Nancy smiled wearily. "You seem to be holding up pretty well," she reasoned.

Ned laughed. "Good night, Nan," he said. "I'll call you in the morning. Drive carefully," he added to George. "Precious cargo."

Bess climbed into the back of Nancy's Mustang, while George took the wheel and Nancy claimed the passenger's seat.

"I thought you were a goner this time," Bess said seriously.

Nancy nodded. "For a while there I thought so, too," she agreed. "Especially when Laurie and I were trapped in that cellar, with the fire getting closer and closer."

"That must have been terrifying," George agreed.

Nancy settled deeper into the seat with a heavy sigh. "And now there are more questions than ever," she muttered. Who tried to kill Laurie? Who started the fire? Would Jon Villiers really have destroyed his own club, whatever the reason? What was he trying to hide? Was Sheila Day alive, or had he murdered her? After all, Nancy had heard Pam call Jon a convicted criminal. Maybe she knew something the rest of them didn't. Why did he lie earlier, saying he hadn't seen or heard from Sheila in two years?

And then Nancy remembered Laurie, helpless in that cellar. Whoever attacked Laurie had failed—which only meant that he would probably try again.

Chapter

Twelve

THE NEXT DAY was bright and sunny, but Nancy woke up in anything but a sunny mood. The case had definitely taken a deadly turn.

She thought about what to do while she showered, dressed, and ate a quick breakfast. Then she was on her way to pick up George. Ned was working for the day and had called to tell Nancy to be careful.

Once George was in the car, Nancy asked for her advice. "Do you suppose Jon will admit anything if I confront him?"

George thought for a moment, then shook her head. "Probably not."

"Well, I'm out of ideas," Nancy said.

"If it's your last hope, give it a shot."

Nancy smiled and turned her car in the direction of the club. There were several official cars in the club's parking lot, along with half a dozen ordinary ones. "Looks like we're not the only ones here to investigate," Nancy said, flipping the engine off and removing the ignition key. From the outside, Moves didn't look too bad. She wondered how extensive the damage was inside.

"I know you, Nan. You were awake half the night trying to figure this out, weren't you?" George asked, looking at the charred building as she spoke.

Nancy nodded. She was feeling sad to think how her conclusions would affect Laurie. "I'm beginning to think Jon set that fire himself," she said, without moving from behind the wheel. "Remember that half-finished letter to his uncle I found in his apartment the other night? And then there was the conversation I overheard outside Jon's office. He needs money fast, and the insurance on Moves might be enough to cover his debt."

"What are you going to do?" George wanted to know. "After all, you can't just walk up to Jon and ask if he's committed arson lately."

Nancy smiled sadly at that. "You're right. But I'm hoping to get him to explain a few other things—like what happened to Sheila Day. He was being evasive last night, George. Sheila wrote to him just two months ago."

George nodded, saying nothing.

"Sheila expected to marry Jon," Nancy said, thinking aloud. "Although her last letter was a little desperate—it sounded as though Jon had asked her to back off for a while—all the dreams and hopes were still there. She even talked about what color the bridesmaids' dresses would be."

George sat up straight in her seat. "Look who's here," she said dryly.

Nancy followed her gaze and saw Brenda Carlton strolling confidently across the parking lot. She was carrying an expensive tape recorder with a microphone. "We'd better hurry," Nancy said, quickly unfastening her seat belt and getting out of the car.

She and George went into Moves by the side entrance. There was charred wood everywhere, but the floor and walls looked relatively solid. The smell of water and burned wood was almost repugnant.

Nancy asked George to distract Brenda for a few minutes while she found Jon and asked him some questions. George agreed, and the two girls went in separate directions.

There were insurance investigators and representatives from the fire department all around. Nancy threaded her way through them until she found Jon.

"This club meant everything to me," Jon was telling a man in a suit. "What reason would I have to destroy it?"

Nancy could think of one reason—to repay the guys he'd borrowed money from—but she didn't say anything. She didn't want Jon to realize how much she knew.

The other man looked at Jon closely. "I'll talk to you again later," he said, and the words carried a warning. "Don't go away."

Nancy stood facing Jon, her hands clasped behind her back. "Have they found out what caused the fire?" she asked.

Jon looked exasperated. "No. But I think they think I set it myself."

Nancy tried not to let her own suspicion show. "What would give them that idea?"

Jon sighed heavily. "There's a lot of money involved," he confessed.

Nancy wanted to pursue that point, but she had to do it carefully. Jon had to trust her, maybe even feel as though he could confide in her. "Is there anything I can do to help?" she asked.

Jon gave her such a grateful smile that she felt a little guilty. "Actually, there is. I've got to pick up some stuff from my apartment. I wouldn't ask you to go for me again, but would you mind just hanging around, keeping an eye on the club while I'm gone?"

Nancy nodded. "No problem." What a golden opportunity to search!

As soon as Jon left, Nancy made her way toward his office. The door was open, so Nancy stepped inside, closing it quietly behind her. The smell of smoke hovered in the air here—but amazingly there was no real harm done to the room itself.

Nancy searched the closet first, finding nothing except an old jacket and a lot of dust. From there, she went to the file cabinet and pulled open the top drawer. One by one, she flipped through every folder but found nothing. She moved on to the next drawer and then the next, with no luck. She almost didn't search the desk, since she'd been through it before, but in the end, her natural curiosity won out. She was so busy that she didn't hear the door open.

"Looking for something?"

Startled, Nancy raised her eyes to see Laurie standing in the doorway, glaring at her. Nancy closed the desk drawer calmly, but her heart was still pounding from the surprise of being caught. She didn't answer Laurie's question, since she wasn't about to lie.

Laurie folded her arms. "It would serve you right if I told Jon the truth—you only took this job so you could spy on him."

Nancy sat on the edge of Jon's desk. "Last

night somebody tried to kill you," she reminded her friend. "It's even possible that the same person came back and shut the cellar door on us, knowing it wouldn't open again. Don't you want to find out what's happening here?"

Laurie bit her lip and closed the door, so that she and Nancy could talk in relative privacy. "Of course I do," she said in an impatient whisper.

"Think back to just before you were hit," Nancy urged. "You must have seen or heard something—or maybe you smelled perfume or cologne—"

But Laurie shook her head resolutely. "There was nothing. I remember being hit and vaguely remember being dragged into the cellar storeroom—whoever did it was strong—but that's all there is." She paused, her eyes round. "I'm scared, Nancy. I'm really scared. There was the noose, and someone tried to drown you at the lake, and now this."

Nancy nodded. "It's serious. Whoever's behind this really means business."

"And you think it's Jon, don't you?" Laurie asked sadly.

Nancy hesitated for a moment. She had no real proof that Jon was guilty of anything. She wasn't going to make an accusation without evidence. "I don't know for sure," she answered. "But things don't look good for Jon. He owes someone a lot of money, Laurie. He's had threats. An insurance check for a burned-out dance club could come in pretty handy right now."

Laurie's soft bangs fluttered against her forehead as she let out her breath. She spread her hands. "What did you hope to find in here, Nancy?" she asked. "A kerosene-soaked rag? A stack of kindling?"

Nancy understood what her friend was feeling. Laurie loved Jon, and she was worried about him—with good reason. "I wasn't looking for anything in particular," Nancy answered carefully. "Sometimes I don't know what I'm trying to find until it turns up."

"And what have you turned up so far?" Laurie pressed.

Before Nancy could dodge that question, the door opened and Jon came in. Once again, Nancy held her breath, expecting Laurie to tell Jon that she'd caught her going through his desk.

"Hi," Laurie said, standing close to Jon and putting her arms around him. "You're having a rough day, aren't you?"

Nancy let out her breath in a sigh.

Jon looked exhausted. "This whole thing is a nightmare." He went around behind the desk and sat down heavily. "The inspector says the fire was set deliberately."

"How?" she asked.

Jon shrugged, rubbing his red eyes with a thumb and forefinger. "They think I did it for the insurance money."

Laurie went to stand behind Jon, rubbing his shoulders. "I know you haven't done anything wrong," she said. Though the words were directed at Jon, Laurie was looking directly at Nancy as she spoke.

"I'll see you later," Nancy said, moving toward the door.

"Thanks for keeping an eye on the place," Jon called after her.

Nancy felt a twinge of guilt as she hurried away. After all, Jon had trusted her, and she'd searched through his personal things.

She found George in the kitchen, which had been badly destroyed, following Brenda Carlton around. Brenda did not look pleased to have the company, but when she saw Nancy, her face lit up.

"I think I know more about this case than you do," she boasted, turning away from the fire inspector she'd been interviewing. "But then, I proved that last night, didn't I?"

Nancy said nothing. She knew Brenda would let information slip if she just kept cool and silent.

"It just so happens that I've found out even more about Jon Villiers," Brenda went on, trying to arouse Nancy's curiosity. She paused, watching Nancy out of the corner of her eye for a reaction.

Nancy managed to look bored. "I don't have time for this," she said, turning and starting to walk away.

The bluff worked. "Jon has an uncle who's done time for burglary," Brenda blurted out. "And he's in bad financial trouble, too."

Nancy turned to face Brenda, waiting.

"Maybe," Brenda rushed on, "Jon burned this place himself. Maybe he wanted the money so he could get out of trouble. And maybe he's about to run off with that pretty little waitress I've seen him chasing after."

A small sound and a movement in the doorway made Nancy, Brenda, and George turn. There in the doorway stood Laurie, her eyes round disks. She had heard it all.

Chapter

Thirteen

LAURIE OBVIOUSLY HEARD EVERYTHING Brenda had said. Apparently she was drawing some painful conclusions. Nancy could see Laurie's mind working—maybe Jon had set the fire. Maybe he was even capable of knocking her out and leaving her to die, she was thinking. But why? What could he hope to gain by it?

While Laurie was still standing there stunned in the doorway of the kitchen, Brenda lifted the camera she was wearing around her neck and snapped a picture. Laurie blinked, temporarily blinded by the flash, then turned and stumbled away.

Nancy started to follow Laurie, but Brenda stepped in front of her, blocking the door. "I'll talk to you later!" Nancy said angrily, pushing past Brenda.

"Don't worry about a thing," Brenda called after Nancy, her voice brimming with fake sweetness. "I'll have the arson figured out by the time you get back."

Nancy ignored Brenda's taunt and hurried outside to the parking lot. Laurie was just getting into her red Mustang.

"Laurie, wait!" Nancy shouted.

Laurie paused long enough to give Nancy a single confused look of defiance and pain. Then she got behind the wheel of her car. Before Nancy could reach the car, the engine roared to life. Laurie's tires squealed against the asphalt as she jammed the gearshift into reverse.

"Laurie!" Nancy called again, really frightened now.

The red Mustang passed Nancy and picked up speed as Laurie moved it out of the parking lot and headed for the main road.

Nancy ran for her own car. Moments later she was following Laurie. This was all Brenda's fault, she thought, as she chased her friend along the highway. If anything happened to Laurie . . .

Nancy stopped herself from thinking that way. Instead, she concentrated on keeping Laurie in sight, silently urging her friend to stop.

Laurie was just ahead, driving carelessly. She weaved back and forth across the center line, and when she came to a turn, she swerved far into the other lane.

Nancy was holding her breath, afraid to take her eyes from the road or the car ahead.

"Laurie, please slow down," she whispered. There was a particularly sharp curve coming up, and, as Nancy had feared, Laurie again swerved wide of the double yellow lines. But this time she found herself roaring head on toward an enormous truck.

Nancy's heart rose into her throat as she watched. The truck's horn screamed a warning, and Laurie's car veered wildly to the right back across the road. It slammed through a white board fence and dead into a tree.

"Oh, *no!*" Nancy cried.

Both Nancy and the truck driver stopped as quickly as they could, but it was Nancy who reached Laurie's car first. The front of the Mustang was crumpled in, and there was steam coming from under the hood.

At least Nancy hoped it was steam, and not smoke.

Through the window, she could see Laurie slumped over the wheel. Nancy frantically grabbed at the car door and yanked, but it wouldn't give.

Just as the truck driver reached the Mustang,

Nancy was running around the car to try the other door. Like the one on the driver's side, it was jammed.

"I called for help on the CB," the truck driver said, pulling to get the door open. "The police will be here any minute, along with an ambulance." He was a big man, as tall as Ned, with well-developed muscles, but he was no more successful at freeing Laurie than Nancy had been.

Nancy pounded on the windshield in a desperate attempt to get some reaction from Laurie. Again and again she called her friend's name.

The front of the car was folded accordion-style, and the white clouds were still escaping from under the hood.

"Is it going to catch on fire?" Nancy asked, her heart beating double-time at the prospect.

The name Fred was stitched on the pocket of the driver's shirt. "I don't think so," he said, turning and running for his truck.

In the far distance Nancy could hear the first strains of sirens. Please hurry, she pleaded silently.

Fred returned carrying a crowbar. Working swiftly and skillfully, he began prying at the door on Laurie's side.

An ambulance and a police car rounded the curve just then, squealing to a stop behind the truck. Fred got the door open when Nancy had to step aside so that the paramedics could free Laurie from her seat belt.

Nancy bit down hard on her lower lip as she waited.

A young police officer appeared beside her. "What happened here, miss?" she wanted to know.

Nancy could see that Laurie's head was bleeding. She wanted to rush up and demand to know whether her friend was all right or not, but she knew how important it was to let the paramedics do their jobs. Laurie's life was hanging in the balance.

Nancy took a deep breath. Never taking her eyes off Laurie, she answered the police officer's question. "Her name is Laurie Weaver, and she's my friend. She was upset and was driving a little recklessly. She came around that curve back there in the wrong lane and to avoid colliding with the truck swerved and crashed into this tree."

They were lifting Laurie out of the car and putting her on a gurney, and Nancy couldn't believe how still Laurie was lying. Her skin was as pale and luminous as wax, her forehead bleeding. She didn't look as if she was alive.

Nancy turned her eyes to one of the paramedics, forcing herself to speak calmly. "Please tell me," she said quietly, "is my friend all right?"

Neither answered. The two men were completely absorbed with Laurie. While Nancy watched, one of them pressed an oxygen mask to Laurie's face and the other hooked her up to an IV.

Nancy pressed closer. "Laurie?"

Laurie didn't move a muscle or make a sound. Nancy could see her friend's chest rising and falling, but that didn't mean she was breathing on her own. The paramedic was giving her oxygen.

"You'll have to stay back, miss," one of them said to Nancy in a kind voice.

Nancy retreated another step. "Laurie?" she said again.

But Laurie didn't stir. She just lay there. Nancy felt tears springing to her eyes.

Would Laurie ever wake up?

Chapter

Fourteen

THEN, SUDDENLY, a strangled whisper came from Laurie's throat, filling Nancy with relief.

Laurie was regaining consciousness!

The paramedic spoke as he and his companion lifted the gurney and carried Laurie quickly to the ambulance. "She's waking up," he said, "but she's not out of danger."

Nancy understood only too well. "Can I ride with her?" she asked, watching as Laurie was lifted into the back of the ambulance.

The paramedic nodded. "That would probably be a good idea. Talk to your friend and try to keep her awake. She may have a concussion."

Nancy scrambled quickly into the back of the ambulance and knelt beside Laurie. The other paramedic was hooking Laurie up to equipment that would monitor her vital signs.

"What happened?" Laurie asked in a small, frightened voice.

"You had an accident," Nancy answered, gently touching Laurie's hand. "You were upset by Brenda Carlton and what she said about Jon, remember? You got into your car—"

Laurie closed her eyes as the memories returned. "I remember now," she said. "Was anyone else hurt?"

Nancy shook her head. "No," she answered.

"I nearly collided with a truck."

Nancy nodded.

"But the driver's all right?"

Again, Nancy nodded. A huge lump was rising on Laurie's forehead, but the paramedic had managed to stop the bleeding.

"I shouldn't have been so careless," Laurie managed to say. "I tried to stop on the highway when I saw you behind me, but—"

Nancy's hand tightened around Laurie's. "You tried to stop?" she asked, not sure that she'd heard right.

There was a dazed expression in Laurie's eyes. "I kept pumping the brakes, but they were gone." She closed her eyes again. "I was so scared, Nancy."

"I know," Nancy answered. Though her voice was calm, her mind was racing. Had someone tampered with Laurie's brakes? But who?

They reached the hospital as Nancy kept turning that question over in her mind. Laurie was wheeled into the emergency room, and Nancy went directly to the telephone to call Laurie's parents.

Mrs. Weaver arrived first, since she'd been at home. She was dressed in her gardening clothes, and her eyes were wide with worry. "What happened?" she cried, clutching Nancy's hands.

Nancy explained quietly and clearly. When Mr. Weaver dashed in a few seconds later Nancy had to tell the story again.

There was nothing Nancy could do at the hospital, so she left and walked a few blocks to a nearby towing company. Within minutes, she was back at the scene of the accident.

The tow truck driver shook his head as he assessed the damage to Laurie's car. "It looks like a total loss to me," he said.

Nancy had no doubt that he was right. "Would you mind checking to see if the brakes have been tampered with?" she asked.

The mechanic gave a curious look, but he dropped to his knees and looked beneath the car. A minute passed before he answered, "Yep. Somebody cut the brakelines, real neat and tidy."

Nancy had hoped that her guess was wrong,

but the tow truck driver had just confirmed her worst suspicions.

She gave the driver Laurie's address and phone number and walked to her own car. "Thanks," she called, before getting behind the wheel.

Knowing George would be really worried, Nancy drove straight back to Moves. George was waiting in the parking lot, and she slid into the passenger seat the moment Nancy stopped.

"Did you catch up with Laurie?" George asked.

Nancy sighed. "Sort of. She crashed through a fence, George, and she's in the hospital right now."

George stopped in the middle of fastening her seat belt. She looked shocked. "Is she all right?"

"I'm not sure," Nancy answered. "She was conscious. Her parents are with her now."

"Did you see what happened?"

"Yes," Nancy answered, the memory filling her mind. "Laurie was driving too fast, but she told me that she tried to stop when she saw me behind her. The brakelines were cut, George—I had the tow truck driver check."

George gasped. "This person is playing for keeps. Whoever it is. Any ideas?"

"It could be Jon. There's a lot of evidence piling up against him. But it was *Adam* I saw inside the club, during the fire. I know I decided he was innocent, but now I can't help thinking that he might have dumped Laurie in that cellar just before I got to him. And Ned told me once that Adam enjoys working on cars—he'd know how to cut a brakeline."

They were passing the place where Laurie had gone through the fence. The tow truck was still there, backed up to Laurie's car. George seemed deep in thought.

"Jon could have done it—or paid someone else to take care of it for him," she suggested after a long time.

Nancy nodded. "You're right," she said, thinking of all the reasons she had to suspect Jon Villiers. He'd lied on several occasions. He had a criminal record. He was in debt. In fact, considering what he might get from the insurance, it was entirely possible that he'd tried to burn down his own club. He'd tried to break up with Laurie once, and there was—or had been—something going on between him and Pam Hastings.

Still, Nancy sensed that Jon cared for Laurie. Deeply.

"Basically," she told George, "we're back to square one. Somebody is either trying to kill Laurie or scare her away, and we still don't know who that somebody is. Or why they're doing it."

"We'll find out," George said confidently, but she looked a little doubtful.

Within minutes they were pulling into the hospital parking lot.

"Are you going to tell Laurie's parents about the brakelines?" George asked.

"I have to tell the police," Nancy replied. "They'll probably pass the word on to the Weavers."

George nodded her agreement as they entered the emergency room and stepped up to the desk.

"We're friends of Laurie Weaver's," Nancy said to the nurse in charge. "Could you please tell us how she's doing?"

The nurse flipped through a stack of cards until she found one with Laurie's name on it. "Laurie is being admitted—for observation."

"What room is she in?" Nancy asked.

"You'd have to ask the clerk at the admitting desk about that," the nurse answered. "It's upstairs, first floor."

"Thank you," Nancy said. She and George found the elevator and went up one floor.

Nancy was getting Laurie's room number when George muttered, "Look who's here."

Nancy lifted her eyes and saw Adam Boyd being pushed out of an elevator in a wheelchair. Both of his hands were bandaged, but he was fully dressed.

"Adam!" Leaving the admitting desk, Nancy walked over to greet him.

"Hi," he said, smiling at Nancy and George. The nurse who had been pushing his wheelchair left for a moment to speak with one of the clerks at the main desk.

"Are you going home today?" Nancy asked. The concern in her voice was genuine.

Adam nodded. "Not a moment too soon, either," he answered. "I was here all night. I hate this place."

George was looking at his bandages. "How bad are the burns?"

He shrugged. "I'll be okay in a few weeks," he said. "They kept me here because of smoke inhalation, mostly."

Nancy and George exchanged a look, then Nancy placed a hand on Adam's shoulder. "Get well soon, okay?" she said.

"Okay," Adam replied, looking pleased at the attention.

"You didn't say anything about Laurie's accident," George commented, when she and Nancy walked away.

"Miss Weaver is in room three hundred seven," the clerk told them when they reached the desk.

"Thank you," Nancy said to her. They were back in the elevator, moving toward the third floor, when she answered George. "There was no point in trying to get a reaction out of Adam," she said. "He couldn't have been the one to cut Laurie's brakeline. He was here all night. So why upset him? I'm sure he could do without more bad news."

The elevator whisked to a stop on the third floor, and Nancy and George stepped out into the hallway. Nurses and doctors bustled past, looking busy and efficient.

They found Laurie propped up on her pillows, her head bandaged. Her skin was pale and she looked tired, but she smiled when she saw Nancy and George. Her father had already left, and Mrs. Weaver slipped out to go to the cafeteria for coffee.

"Hi," George said to Laurie, going to stand at the foot of her bed. "How are you feeling?"

Laurie smiled sadly. "Not so good, actually. When I think of what could have happened—"

Nancy touched Laurie's shoulder. "You were lucky," she said.

Laurie settled back, lifting a hand to her head and wincing with pain. "That depends on your viewpoint," she replied. "You're sure the other driver is all right?"

"He's fine," Nancy answered.

"And my car?"

Now it was Nancy who winced. "It's on its way to the shop. I'm not sure whether it can be repaired or not."

Laurie smiled sadly. "I guess I really blew it this time," she said.

Before Nancy or George could answer, a nurse came in with a pill for Laurie to take. It seemed like a good time to leave, so the girls said goodbye to their friend and left the room.

"What now?" George asked.

Nancy sighed. "Adam was the only real suspect I had besides Jon. So I guess that leaves only one choice."

They took the elevator downstairs and walked out of the building, hurrying across the parking lot to Nancy's car.

"I think I'll go for a drive—I really need to sort all this out," Nancy said, as they pulled out into afternoon traffic. "Want to come along?"

George shook her head. "I'd like to, but I've got some stuff to do at home."

Nancy dropped George off at her house and then set out for the lake. She turned on the radio. A familiar love song rolled out of the speakers, its melody sad and romantic. Now, where had she heard that song recently?

Ahead of Nancy, the traffic light turned red. She coasted to a halt. Why did she feel so completely wrong about this case? Why was it that she couldn't bring herself to believe—really believe, in her heart—that Jon Villiers could be a cold-blooded killer? All the evidence pointed to him and no one else.

As the light changed, Nancy gripped the steering wheel tightly. I have to talk to him, she realized. I have to lay it all out, give him a chance to explain.

Taking a deep breath, Nancy swung into a right turn and headed for Moves. She hoped her instincts were right.

Because if she were wrong, she was playing right into the hands of a murderer.

Chapter

Fifteen

THERE WERE ONLY TWO CARS left in the parking lot at Moves as Nancy arrived. Nancy parked near the kitchen entrance to the club, thinking she'd find Jon in his office. The small room was empty, so Nancy picked her way through the debris of the fire until she reached the dance floor.

Jon was in the sound booth, frowning as he appeared to be examining the expensive equipment. When he saw Nancy, he gave her a weary smile.

"Hi," he said, stepping out to speak with her.

"I'm afraid it'll be a while before we can open the club for business again. I've had to let all the waitresses go temporarily—"

"I didn't come here about my job," Nancy broke in quietly, folding her arms. It was time to be honest with Jon. "I have to ask you some serious questions, Jon—and I need straight answers."

"This sounds pretty important," Jon replied with a weary grin. "Let's talk in my office." He paused to look around at what remained of his club. "It's about the only place in the building that wasn't burned to a crisp."

Nancy led the way back to Jon's office and sat down in a chair facing him while he took a seat behind his desk. His elbows on the desktop, he made a steeple of his fingers and sat back to wait for Nancy to begin.

She took a deep breath to prepare herself. This could be unpleasant. "Who was the man who was in here last night, just before the fire?" she asked finally. "I heard him tell you to 'pay up or get the job done.'"

Jon's face darkened. "So Pam was right. You *were* here to snoop," he muttered.

Nancy leaned forward in her chair. "This situation has gotten really dangerous," she said. "If I can't get answers from you, I'm going to have to go to the police."

"Don't do that," Jon said quickly. "I'll tell you everything you want to know."

Nancy watched him, waiting calmly for an answer to her original question.

Jon sighed. "The man you heard was my uncle, Mike Rivers."

"And?" Nancy prompted after a long time.

Jon became reticent to continue. "We were only talking business," he said, glaring at her.

Nancy decided then and there to let him know all her suspicions. "What job did your uncle want you to get done? How did he get out of the fire? That day of Laurie's party, when you were talking to someone on the telephone in Mr. Weaver's study, you promised to 'take care of her.' Who was the 'her' you were going to take care of, and what were you going to do? Was the deep-fryer 'accident' just a dress rehearsal for last night's fire?" She paused to take a breath. "Were all your problems just going to go up in smoke, Jon— including Laurie?"

Jon was staring at Nancy in amazement all the while she talked, but her last question seemed to break down the wall he'd been hiding behind.

"I came to River Heights hoping to make a fresh start," he explained angrily. His frustration was obvious to Nancy. "I really needed to get away from Chicago and shake off my past, and I had a good idea—Moves. Unfortunately, I didn't have the money it took to get a club like this going."

"So you borrowed," Nancy guessed.

Jon nodded sadly. "I went to some friends of my uncle's," he confessed. "From the very first, they've been waiting for me to blow it so they can step in and take over—run it their way, with some illegal gambling to liven things up a little. Moves has turned a profit since I opened it, though, and I've always been able to make the payments on the loan. There's only one left, in fact."

Nancy sat in silence while Jon struggled with some inner emotion that prevented him from going on.

Finally, he began again. "I haven't been able to come up with that last payment, since the last quarter's taxes were higher than I expected. That's the money you heard my uncle demanding last night."

Nancy nodded, urging Jon to keep talking.

"As for the job he referred to," Jon went on, "that was a little scheme he came up with to help me meet the payment and get those loan sharks off my back." His face twisted with self-disgust. "He wanted me to case the Weavers' house, so he could rob it."

Nancy remembered Brenda Carlton telling her that Jon's uncle was a convicted burglar. It all clicked. "But you refused?"

"I really care about Laurie," Jon said hotly, meeting Nancy's eyes.

Nancy decided not to test him on that yet. There were other things she needed to find out first. "What about the fire? Did you set it?"

The expression in his eyes was bleak. "No," he said, in a forceful whisper. "This place was the best chance I had of making something out of my life."

Nancy asked, "How about your uncle? Could he have done something like this? He was around just before the fire, Jon, and then I didn't see him again."

"He left the minute he smelled smoke," Jon answered. "He didn't want to be here when the police arrived. And before that, he was with me."

"Then who did it?" Nancy pressed.

Jon raked his fingers through his hair in a gesture of frustration. "I don't know," he said. "But I know one thing—I'm going to get the blame because of my record. Because of a stupid thing I did when I was a kid."

"The insurance inspectors still think you set the fire?" Nancy prodded.

Jon nodded. "I'm looking at a long stretch in prison for arson and insurance fraud, and I'm not guilty!" he said angrily.

Nancy was beginning to believe Jon. He was smart—he'd have known that the insurance people would suspect him of arson, and that it would be hard to collect his money. But even more than that, Nancy believed he wouldn't destroy the club that meant so much to him.

"Let's go back to the idea of casing the Weavers' house for a burglary," she said. "Was that what you were talking about in Laurie's father's study during her party?"

"I was trying to stall," Jon confessed. "But, at the same time, I had to pretend that I would go along with the robbery. I figured if I could come up with the money I needed some other way, there would be no need to steal from the Weavers. When I said I'd 'take care of her,' I meant I'd make sure Laurie was out of the house when the time came."

"I see." Nancy nodded for him to continue.

"I didn't want Laurie to be hurt in any way," Jon said miserably. "I tried to break off with her—I thought that would get my uncle off my back about robbing her family. After all, if I wasn't seeing Laurie, how could I be the finger man for a burglary?"

"But you went on seeing Laurie," Nancy pointed out.

Jon's shoulders moved in a forlorn shrug. "Right from the first moment I saw Laurie, I was crazy about her," he said. "Giving her up was too hard. Especially since she didn't want me to."

"And Pam? What's going on with her?"

Jon's lips formed a tight line for a moment before he answered, "Nothing. Not a thing."

"I've seen you together, Jon," Nancy told him. "Maybe you aren't involved with Pam now, but you have been."

Jon looked away, unwilling to meet Nancy's eyes. "I told you, there's nothing going on," he said forcefully. Nancy didn't press him—she knew she'd hit a brick wall. It was clear that Jon wasn't going to say another word on the subject.

"All right, it's nothing," Nancy said, echoing his words. "What about Sheila Day? Was that nothing, too? Why did you lie about her?"

Jon stared at Nancy as though she'd sprouted an extra set of eyes. "Sheila? You mean you don't—" He broke off abruptly. There was a wary look in his eyes. "Sheila's not involved in this. I assure you, she's very much alive. I've got problems with her, but she has no part in what's been going on."

Nancy let the subject drop. "Did you know I found Laurie unconscious on the cellar floor last night? She didn't get there by accident— somebody struck her over the head and took her down there to die in the fire. Do you think your uncle could have taken matters into his own hands and tried to get Laurie out of the way?"

Jon didn't hesitate for a moment. He immediately shook his head. "Uncle Mike might steal, but he'd never kill anybody. And why would he kill his meal ticket? Without Laurie he wouldn't learn any more about the Weavers."

Jon riffled through the papers on his desk until he found a check. "Here," he said, extending it to Nancy. "This is yours."

Nancy shook her head. She hadn't taken the job at Moves for money, and they both knew it now. Accepting payment wouldn't be right. "Give it to charity or something," she said.

Jon laid the check down and leaned forward in his chair. "She—" He stopped and moistened his lips. "Pam was suspicious about you from the first, you know," he told her. "She wanted me to fire you. I'm glad I didn't, though—I'm really glad I didn't."

"Why?" Nancy asked, honestly puzzled. She was about to leave and had risen out of her chair.

"Because if I had, you wouldn't have been here to save Laurie from the fire. I'll always be grateful that you got Laurie out in time."

Nancy winced. That brought her to the one topic she hadn't discussed yet: Laurie's accident. Briefly, she explained how Laurie had gotten upset and wrecked her Mustang.

"Somebody cut her brakeline," she finished, watching Jon carefully.

"What?" Jon choked out, shooting up from his chair.

Nancy held up a hand. "She's all right! They're only keeping her overnight for observation," she said.

Jon didn't even hear her. Looking as though he'd just seen a ghost, he pushed past Nancy and raced out of the office at a dead run.

Chapter

Sixteen

NANCY REMAINED in the small, cluttered office for a few moments after Jon had left, thinking. As far as she was concerned, another suspect had just been ruled out. Whatever Jon Villiers might have lied about, whatever he'd done, he wasn't behind the attacks on Laurie—he cared too much. And they would serve no purpose.

Nibbling at her lower lip, a frown furrowing her brow, Nancy stepped out into the hallway.

Who was left to suspect? Now that she'd ruled out Adam Boyd—he'd been in the hospital with two injured hands when Laurie's brakeline was cut—and Jon himself, there seemed to be no one with a real motive.

There was Jon's uncle Mike, but that was unlikely. The attacks on Laurie seemed, at the very least, geared to driving her away from Moves and Jon. Nancy knew that would be the last thing Jon's uncle would want. The more Laurie loved and trusted Jon, the more it would suit the older man's purposes.

What about Pam? There was definitely something between Pam and Jon. Maybe it was in the past, but . . .

"Wait a minute. Wait a minute!" Nancy whispered as an incredible idea suddenly struck her.

What if she'd been on the right track when she'd thought Adam Boyd was behind all the mischief? He and Laurie had loved each other in the past, and he was jealous of Laurie and Jon.

But Nancy took the idea one step further. Laurie and Adam weren't the only ones with a past. What about Jon and Pam? More to the point, what about Jon and Sheila Day?

Nancy had assumed that Sheila was out of the picture—that she was still in Chicago, where she and Jon had been dance partners. Nancy had been guessing that Jon had come to River Heights partly to get away from Sheila. He met Pam right away, then dropped her as soon as he met Laurie.

143

But if Pam and Jon had dated for such a short time, why did they seem to know each other so well? The times Nancy had seen them together, there had been a connection between them that could only come from knowing each other a long time.

And they danced together so perfectly. . . .

What was it Jon had said? "She—Pam was suspicious about you from the first." Now, there was an interesting slip of the tongue. Could he have been about to say, *"Sheila* was suspicious about you . . ."?

In fact, what if Sheila Day had been in River Heights all along? What if she was the one trying to kill Laurie? It would make perfect sense. . . .

From the main part of the club came the soft strains of a slow song. Nancy nodded to herself. Right on cue, she thought.

Quickly and quietly, she made her way to the doors and slipped inside the dancing area, being careful to keep to the shadows.

Pam Hastings was standing in the center of the enormous, burned-out room. As Nancy watched, she set a large portable radio down on the floor beside her. Music flowed from its speakers.

Pam was dressed in jeans, a T-shirt, and a lightweight jacket. Even in the poor light, Nancy could see the wild glint of emotion in the girl's eyes.

Facing her, his hands in his pockets, was Jon.

Nancy was surprised, since he'd been in such a hurry to leave the club and see Laurie.

"For once, Jon Villiers," Pam was saying, "you're going to listen to me. I love you. I'm the only woman who can make you happy."

Jon's answer confirmed all Nancy's suspicions. "Sheila, give it up," he said quietly. "Please."

Sheila Day—alias Pam Hastings—stepped toward Jon, holding out her arms, as the music continued. "Let's dance, like we used to. We had a good thing going."

"We did," Jon agreed, his voice steely, "but I told you again and again—it's over. You and I are through."

Sheila shook her head. "You don't understand. I did it all for you—I did so many things for you."

Jon's shoulders slumped as if a great weight had suddenly fallen on them. "Like what?" he asked wearily, barely listening.

Sheila shrugged her shoulders and spread her hands. "All of it. The slashed tires."

"So that was really aimed at Laurie, not Nancy," Jon guessed, suddenly more alert.

Sheila nodded. "They both have Mustangs—I got them mixed up."

"What else have you done?" Jon asked.

As Nancy watched, Sheila seemed to puff up with pride. "I left a noose on Laurie's porch, and I held that nosy Nancy Drew under the water at the lake, too. She never learns, you know. When that didn't work, I arranged the grease 'accident' in the kitchen—to scare her off."

Nancy saw Jon shudder slightly. "And you're responsible for this, too?" he asked, indicating the burned-out club with a wave of one hand.

Sheila shrugged. "You didn't give me a choice, Jon. I tried to talk to you, but you wouldn't listen. I had to do something big, don't you see?"

Jon simply stared at her, stunned by what she'd done.

Sheila went on, almost proudly. "I knew you'd love me again, if I could just get Laurie out of the way. We need to get away from here, you and I, make a new start. I decided to kill two birds with one stone, if you'll excuse the expression. I hit Laurie over the head and dragged her into the cellar, then I set the fire." She paused, and a frown altered her features. "Everything would have been okay, if it hadn't been for Nancy Drew. By rights, she and Laurie both should have gone up in smoke."

Jon was shaking his head in amazement. "You're crazy," he muttered.

Sheila's eyes shone with tears. "That's right," she answered, sounding a little worried. "Crazy about you."

Jon started to leave. "I've got to get to Laurie," he said.

Sheila immediately stepped in front of him.

"No," she said. "There is no Laurie, not anymore. I cut the brakelines in her car—it's too late. She's dead."

"Get out of my way," Jon said, through gritted teeth. It looked to Nancy as though he was just barely able to control his temper, disgust, and horror.

"She's alive?" Sheila asked, in a whisper.

"She's alive," Jon confirmed furiously. He would have pushed past Sheila and gone then—except that she pulled an automatic pistol from the pocket of her jacket and pointed it at him.

"You're not going to her," she breathed.

Jon stood completely still, his eyes on the gun. "Sheila, give it up. Enough people have been hurt."

"You're not going to her," Sheila repeated.

Jon took a step toward her. Sheila pulled back the hammer. "You really mean it, don't you?" she whispered brokenly. "You want her, not me."

"Sheila—"

"I'm going to kill you," Sheila said, pointing the gun directly at Jon's chest. "Goodbye, Jon."

Chapter

Seventeen

JON HELD UP both hands in a useless effort to protect himself. "Sheila, don't," he whispered desperately.

She laughed. "It's too late," she said, holding the gun in both hands and waving it wildly from side to side. "Do you hear me? It's too late! You don't love me anymore—you love her!" For a moment pain twisted Sheila's features, but then she was smiling again. "I was hoping to get you back, I admit that—but I had this backup plan."

Jon said nothing. His hands remained in midair, and his eyes were still fixed on the pistol.

Nancy, meanwhile, was inching her way closer, moving silently through the shadows.

"You know," Sheila went on, "you've gone soft since the old days, when we used to work with Mike. I should have seen it before. You're nothing but a—a coward."

Jon moistened his lips. He had every reason to be scared, but he was keeping his head. Nancy admired him for that.

Hold on! she thought as she slipped between charred tables and chairs.

"Give me the gun, Sheila," Jon said, cautiously holding out his hand. "We'll talk. Somehow, we'll work everything out."

Sheila shook her head. "That isn't going to work. I know you're only trying to get the gun away."

Nancy held her breath as Jon took another step toward Sheila.

"You don't want to kill me," he said.

"Yes, I do," Sheila argued. "That was plan B—killing you for the insurance money and starting over somewhere else. I'd be lonely, but I'd be rich, too."

"What insurance money?" Jon asked, frowning.

Again, Sheila gave that chilling laugh. "You have a terrible memory, darling," she said. "Remember when we were engaged, and you took

149

out that policy on your life so I'd be provided for if something happened to you?"

Jon nodded slowly, looking baffled.

"Well," Sheila boasted, "I've kept up the premiums. Now, Jon darling, I'm going to collect."

"Collect?" Jon echoed. "You won't get a penny, Sheila—you'll be in jail for murder."

Easy, Nancy thought. Don't get her excited.

Sheila shook her head. "I'll clean out the office safe before I go—the police will think you were killed by burglars."

Nancy was closer than before, but she was still too far away to stop Sheila. Seeing her raise the pistol, she grabbed a sooty soda glass from a table and hurled it behind Sheila, in order to distract her.

When Sheila whirled, startled by the sound, Nancy rushed toward her, grappling for the gun.

"No!" Sheila screamed, hatred in her eyes.

The girls struggled and the pistol discharged once before Nancy finally wrested it from Sheila's grip.

Jon came up behind Sheila and caught her by the arms when she tried to lunge at Nancy again. His face filled with sadness, he again said the words that had driven Sheila to despair in the first place.

"It's over."

* * *

Nancy, George, and Bess were all crowded around Laurie's bed as Nancy explained the case.

"So all along it was Pam—Sheila—doing those awful things," Laurie said. "Is she in jail?"

Nancy nodded. "Jon called the police and, when they got there, Sheila confessed to everything."

Just then, Jon stepped into the room. There was a resolute expression on his face. Nancy thought she knew what he had come for. Poor Jon, she thought. And poor Laurie, too.

"We'll see you later," George said to Laurie, taking Bess by the arm and starting toward the door. Nancy was right behind them.

"Please don't go," Jon said. "I want all of you to hear this."

The three girls stopped and turned to look at Jon and then Laurie.

"I'm leaving River Heights," he announced. "At least for a while."

Laurie looked alarmed for a moment, but then she lowered her eyes and Nancy guessed that she was relieved, as well as sad.

Jon cupped his hand under Laurie's chin and kissed her lightly on the forehead. "It's because I care about you so much that I want to go away," he said softly, his voice full of tenderness. "Too much has happened—we both need time to think about what we really feel. I'll be back someday, Laurie, and if you still want me, we can start again."

Laurie nodded sadly. After kissing her once again, very gently, Jon left the room without looking back.

Nancy, George, and Bess clustered around Laurie's bed once more. Tears glimmered in her eyes, but she was trying hard to smile.

"I'll bet he really will be back someday," she said.

"I think you may be right," Nancy agreed, smiling at her friend. "Who can tell what the future holds?"

Nancy's next case:

Film star Brady Armstrong is in River Heights for the premiere of his newest movie at the grand old Century Cinema. When Nancy's friend Bess decides to go backstage to see her heartthrob, she stumbles into a kidnapping meant for the movie actor.

But the kidnapper doesn't want ransom money. He demands that the planned demolition of the Century Cinema theater be halted—or Bess will be destroyed with it. Unable to prevent the wreckers from tearing down the building, Nancy races against time to discover where Bess is hidden—and unmask the mysterious figure who is dead set on stealing the show . . . in *THE FINAL SCENE,* Case #38 in The Nancy Drew Files™.